The Sixties Boys

The Sixties Boys

Alan Hammond

Millstream Books

This book is dedicated to my family and friends,
past and present,
who in one way or another have had an influence on my life.

The stories in the book are based on the life, experiences and memories of the author and others. All names of people, places and dates have been changed. Individuals shown in the photographs are not related to any of the story lines.

The group's name, 'Modern Edge', and the composition 'Suburban Mod' are not meant to represent any particular band with this name or any song with this title; they are purely names invented for the storyline of this book.

First published in 2009 by Millstream Books, 18 The Tyning, Bath BA2 6AL

Set in Adobe Jensen Pro

Printed in Great Britain by Short Run Press Limited, Exeter, Devon

Text © Alan Hammond 2009
Front cover photograph © Glyn Grainger
Rear cover photograph © Christine Hammond

ISBN 978 0 948975 88 2

British Library Cataloguing-in-Publication Data:
a catalogue record for this book is available from the British Library

Contents

Foreword

I am very pleased to write this foreword for Alan's new book which mirrors some of my own experiences in bands.

In 1960 I was doing a double act with my best mate from school, Dave Bramley. My name at the time was Anthony Fitzgerald – still is I suppose. Anyway we decided that we needed to go out as brothers, thinking that our own christian names were not snazzy enough, and we decided to pick a name out of the telephone directory. I closed my eyes, opened the book at a random page, stuck my finger on it, and it was on the name Grant. From that moment on we became the Grant Brothers.

Our first paid gig was as a support act to the great comedian Norman Collier. Also on the bill was a young singer called Lynne Perry, who later found fame as Ivy Tilsley in *Coronation Street*. The name of the venue was the Conisbrough Ivanhoe WMC and the actual stage is featured on the front cover of my album, *Made in Sheffield*.

When Dave lost interest in show business (by now he was more interested in girls than music), I carried on as a solo singer until I was offered a job in a group called *The Counterbeats*. I know it's a terrible name, but back then it was considered quite hip! The reason for me joining them was because their lead singer, a girl called Karen Young, had left them and had just made a record called *Nobody's Child*, which had gone straight to Number One in the charts.

I carried on fronting several more bands throughout the sixties with much more success on the cabaret club circuit, until I was spotted at the Winter Gardens in Blackpool by Harvey Lisberg, who had discovered Peter Noone and Herman's Hermits, and was now managing 10cc. He introduced me to Mitch Murray and Peter Callander, two very successful songwriters and producers, and we started to have hits around the world.

I'm still in contact with some of the old band members from those sixties days and we reminisce about the great times we had together on the road. It's funny but all the bad times that we had are put to the back of the mind as though they didn't happen. All those mind-numbing hours spent driving up and down the country from the far north of Scotland down to Wales, and staying in some really bad digs or caravan parks and eating at roadside cafés. Once, on the way from Doncaster to go down to Wales, a pebble went through the windscreen in the driving rain. We had to carry on driving with no windscreen, all the way from Leicester to the Welsh valleys; there was no motorway system then. When we arrived, we were all soaked to the skin and frozen to death. I went on stage and opened my mouth and nothing came out. I lost my voice for four days. No gig, no money. Happy Days?

Tony Christie

Introduction & Acknowledgements

They say if you remember the sixties you weren't there. Well I remember it like it was yesterday, it was a magical era to be a teenager. There were bands playing fantastic music round every corner and life was uncomplicated then. We weren't driven by a designer world; if you couldn't afford it, you went without.

I hope this book will put a smile on your face and remind you of what some of us teenagers did back in the sixties. If you weren't there and you are reading this, perhaps this book will give you a taste of those fun days when we didn't have a care in the world.

If you were an early sixties teenager you've now got your bus pass. You will probably be taking your morning blood pressure tablet, and waiting for the postman to deliver that letter from the hospital, to inform you when you can have your hip or knee replaced. You are more than likely looking after your screaming grandchildren and bailing your own kids out. Other than that life is great.

It requires teamwork to publish a book and I've been very lucky to have a great team with me. First of all a special thank-you to Tony Christie for writing the foreword for me. He is not only a great singer and entertainer, but a really nice guy.

I would like to thank my wife Christine for all her encouragement, support and help in the writing of this book. Her contribution in checking the manuscript with her red pen made me wonder if I went to the right school.

A big vote of thanks goes to my publisher, Tim Graham, who has published my previous eleven books, and supported me with this new venture.

Sincere thanks go to my best mate, Terry Page, who has jogged my memory about those sixties days, and has added some of his own thoughts and ideas.

My good friend John Clifton has been of great assistance in enthusiastically copy-editing the manuscript and adding a few memories of his own.

Special mention and thanks go to Judy Hall who's done more than her call of duty with the proof-reading and editing of the book. I am also very grateful to Frances Bristow, Peter Day, and Richard Derry for all their diligent proof-reading and advice.

My heartiest thanks must go to Allan Stanistreet who first read the draft, and put me right on so many things.

Many others have made important contributions to the book; they include Graham Hickman, Sandra Page, Carole Clifton, Eleanor Roberts, Michelle Hammond, Eric Hammond, Bryn Owen, Victor McCullough, Gary Hall, Walthamstow Memories Site, Roger Curd, Glyn Grainger, Lucia Jordan of the Vespa Club, Chris Hayes, Herby Boxall, Pat Bodin, Colin Caddy, Colin Howard, James Truett (of Jaywalk Music in Street), Robert Jeeves (of Step Back In Time in Brighton), Chris Dyer, Dave Nelhams, Marcus Blackman, Alan Grieve, Brian Rushgrove, Ian Gussey, Tony Thompson, Michael Welch, Tony Green and Graham Marshall.

As one or two photographs are from people's private collections a reader may well recognise a photograph that they took themselves. We offer our apologies in advance for not being able to credit you in person.

1964

Radio Caroline broadcasts from the North Sea.
The head of the Little Mermaid statue in Copenhagen is sawn
    off and stolen.
Richard Burton and Elizabeth Taylor are married.
The Singing Nun (Jeanne-Paule Marie Deckers) appears on the
    Ed Sullivan show in America.
The Beatles' first film, A Hard Day's Night, opens.
Nelson Mandela is jailed for life for treason.
Twelve members of the The Great Train Robbery gang are
    sentenced to a total of 307 years in prison.
Nehru, India's Prime Minister, dies of a heart attack.
China explodes its first atomic bomb.
Three women are prosecuted for indecency for wearing topless
    dresses on Westminster Bridge.
Playschool is the first programme broadcast on the new
    television channel, BBC 2.
The first issue of The Sun appears.
Liverpool win Division 1 and West Ham win the FA Cup.
There are two Prime Ministers – Alec Douglas-Home and
    Harold Wilson.
Country music star Jim Reeves dies in an air crash, aged 40.
Cassius Clay takes the world heavyweight boxing title from
    Sonny Liston.
MPs vote 355 to 170 to abolish the death penalty for murder.
Harpo, the silent Marx Brother, dies.
Soul Singer Sam Cooke is shot dead at a Los Angeles motel.
Prince Edward is born.
Top of the Pops is shown for the first time.

1

Where it all Started

The name is Nick Sheldon and I've just been woken up by the clatter of poxy milk bottles, as the milkman takes them out of his milk float on a cold Saturday morning in 1964. I've got a real thumping, sickly head after last night. I suppose after a gallon of Watney's Red Barrel, a packet of Woodbines, and a fish and chip supper with a couple of pickled onions, it's self inflicted. Even so, I put my grey and maroon Dansette record player on and play my new 45 rpm single 'Can't Buy Me Love' by The Beatles. The record cost me 6/8d so it's going to get plenty of plays. I've been buying ex-jukebox records without the middles in them for 1/6d each.

I'm 17, a bit of a Mod, and live in south-east England with my mum, dad and younger brother Arthur. My nickname for him is short arse, after the comedian Arthur Askey. My dad calls him another name, 'depth charge', because he's always after a sub. Our two-bedroom, Victorian terraced house sounds great; unfortunately it's still bomb damaged from the war; well, it feels like it, especially when you go outside to the privy and face the big wooden toilet seat and a large hole. The bog paper is all cut up in squares from Fleet Street's finest, *The Daily Herald*. The squares have a hole through them with a piece of string attached, which is hung on a nail. Hanging on the side of the privy is the tin bath, in which my mum used to bath me in front of the coal fire, when I was a kid. Nearby is the mangle and washboard that my mum still uses. As I make my way out of the house I say goodbye to her as she's listening to *The Archers* on her Bakelite KB radio, which looks like a toaster.

It's haircut day, so I'm off out in my secondhand black Ford 100E motor to see Sid, who does cut a nice Boston. Before the car, I had a Lambretta 125. My mum's a real diamond, she's put a nice shine on my winkle-pickers, and my Ben Sherman shirt is Omo white. On the way I stop at a garage, put two gallons of Cleveland Discol in, and a shot of Redex, which cost me 7/8d; petrol is getting really expensive. I also stop at a newsagent's and buy 20 Woodbines for 3/6d.

I call in at the tyre shop where my best mate Steve works. He's the same age as me and you can trust him with your life. Like me, he loves his football, music and, of course plenty of girls. The tyres on my motor are as bald as a coot, so Steve sorts out four runners for me at half a quid each. He fits the tyres and takes two £1 notes off me – this hurts, as it's two day's pay. We shoot next door to the café for a greasy spoon; even the flies keep well away from here. The radio in the café is playing 'Bits And Pieces' by The Dave Clark Five. After eating our full English, we discuss Saturday night's entertainment.

'Where'd you fancy going tonight, Steve?'

'I've heard there's a great group called Rob Brown and The Chasers playing at Witham. Ronnie and Rod went up there last week, and they said there was crumpet hanging off the wall. I know it's a few miles out, but I think it's worth going.'

'No more to be said, I'll pick you up at 7.30 and be ready, and don't drown yourself in Old Spice, it stinks the bleedin' motor out.'

After leaving Steve and on the way to the barber's, I pass an ice cream parlour called Alfonzo's. We often go there and meet up with the gang and have a coffee and some of their great Italian Rossi ice cream. I always laugh when I pass it; it's where me and Steve met our first proper girlfriends, Shirley and Sue. I was going out with Shirley and at her birthday party had my first real kiss with a girl, unfortunately she fainted. I didn't know whether it was a great kiss, or because I'd just had a blackcurrant Spangle.

'What's wrong with the kiss?' I said.

'It was wet, horrible and my mouth felt like it had been chewed to bits.'

Yeah, it must have been those Spangles!

I arrive at the barber's and I'm greeted by Radio Caroline playing 'Diamonds' by Jet Harris and Tony Meehan on Sid's radio. Radio Caroline first came on air in March 1964, followed later by Radio London. The ships are broadcasting just outside British waters, and are anchored off the coastline in the North Sea, so we get a good reception. There's some great DJs on the 'pirate stations', as they are called, including Simon Dee, Tony Blackburn, 'Spangles' Muldoon, Chris Moore, Dave Lee Travis, Johnnie Walker, Kenny Everett and 'Emperor' Rosko. Sid, the barber, is 60 years old, unshaven and overweight, with bullfrog eyes and yellow teeth. He smokes more fags than a monkey in a laboratory. He smothers himself with British Sterling aftershave which makes you feel sick; he uses a lot so you don't smell his BO. He always tries to get the gory details out of you about your sex life, most of which we make up. With my Boston haircut finished, I get up to leave, and pay him three bob. The bloke next to me was having a Tony Curtis – rather him than me. Sid looks left, then right, and in a low voice with saliva drooling from his mouth he utters those immortal words:

'Anything for the weekend, young Nick?'

He opens the drawer; well there's more Johnnies in there than Boots the Chemist. I have a ferret through and pull out a couple of packets of three.

'You know that all the copies of the novel *Fanny Hill* are being seized as obscene, which is good news for me.'

He then takes me to another cabinet and opens the door. In there are piles and piles of *Fanny Hill*.

'Tell your mates if they want a copy they know where to come.'

❧ ❧ ❧

Later on I picked up Steve. He'd had a change of aftershave; he'd rested the Old Spice and was on Yardley Cologne, which wasn't that much better. We lit up two of his Embassy tipped and were off to Witham for a great night at the dance, run by the local church youth club. Lots of churches around the country had their own youth clubs, and they'd put on live bands; unfortunately no alcohol, just soft drinks like Corona and Tizer. The dances in the sixties included The Shake, Mashed Potato, Funky Chicken, Jive, Locomotion, Hitch-Hike, Frug, Penguin, Hanky Panky, Swim, and Fly. My favourite was The Twist.

The band that night was great and they played plenty of music from The Beatles, The Stones, Billy J. Kramer & The Dakotas, Hollies, Dave Clark Five and The Searchers. As it happens, we did meet a couple of nice girls, Rita and Sandra, from nearby Braintree. They had the old Essex countryside twang and we over-played our secondhand cockney accent to the full, which they loved. As always we fell in love with them for the night. Rita and I were getting on really well and her hair was something else. It was backcombed and frizzed and well lacquered. She wore a pencil skirt and polka dot blouse. Her Apple Blossom perfume sent me wild. We always liked to know what perfume the girls were wearing, as they were well impressed when you first met them and knew the name of their perfume. If I say so myself, I could dance a mean Twist and Rita, to be fair, was a great mover. I'm giving it the full Twist when unfortunately, my size 10 winkle-pickers with zips up the side, caught her ankle, and she fell over. The only plus side was her showing her suspenders and Aristoc stocking tops. I was now definitely in love. Steve and Sandra were taking the piss as I pulled her up off the floor. Fortunately, the next number the band played was a nice slow one called 'I Think Of You' by the Merseybeats, and she forgave me as I nibbled her ear. We met them a few times afterwards, but the five bob petrol money each time we saw them was playing havoc with our cash flow, so we had to call it a day, a wrong move.

It was a real downer later when girls started to wear tights instead of stockings. That bit of mystique had gone and there was no sex appeal in girls wearing horrible tights. All the blokes would be sitting on a bus or train looking at the girl's legs to see whether they were wearing tights or stockings. One of our mates couldn't help himself; it got so bad he was banned by the local bus company.

In life there's always a sting in the tail. A couple of weeks later, me and Steve were having a little flutter in the bookies; we'd just won a couple of quid on a horse called Lucky Boy when one of the punters we knew showed us the front page of one of the early evening newspapers.

'Lucky bugger, winning that £150,000 on the football pools,' he said.

Steve glanced at the headlines, and then pulled the paper off the bloke.

'I don't believe it, look at this Nick. Could that be who I think it is?'

I looked at the headlines and read further down the page. I had to sit down; I couldn't take in what I was reading.

'Well, you've dropped a bollock there, Nick, if I'm right.'

The headline read: 'Mr. B, a 50-year-old rat catcher from Braintree, Essex has won the big one on the football pools.' I knew Rita's old man was 50, because we went to his birthday party. His surname began with B, and he could catch a mean rat. He said to me at the party, while I was drinking a pint of his Worthington 'E', that if there was any funny business with his only daughter Rita, he'd put my vital parts in one of his rat traps! Braintree is a small market town and there can't be too many rat catchers there, it had to be him.

As it was in the evening paper, it wouldn't hit the morning papers until the next day, and she wouldn't know that I knew her family had come into a considerable amount of money, which I'd like to help her spend. We filled up with another five bob's worth of petrol and left for Braintree. I'd bought a big box of Mackintosh Weekend Assortment chocolates and nicked some flowers out of the local park. Now I was in business, an extra splash of my new Brut Cologne by Fabergé, and I was ready to go. My line was I'd made a mistake in packing her in and I was really missing her, and wanted her back, as life without her was unbearable. Of course, Steve was in the motor winding me up.

We arrived and parked around the corner and noticed that the press boys hadn't put two and two together yet. With the flowers and chocolates in my hand I went up the path and knocked on the door, Rita opened it and I went into my patter and handed over the goodies. She seemed impressed, the old Sheldon charm was working. She let me finish and I knew I was back in; I was spending the money already. I'd just about put my foot across the threshold, when she verballed me and went into one. She slammed the door in my face, which bent the ends of my winkle-pickers. I limped painfully back to the motor and sat down behind the wheel, shell-shocked. Steve had a big grin on his face as he handed me a fag.

'It worked then,' he said.

'Oh yeah, two words, first letter, first word F, second word, last letter F.'

What really annoyed me was she'd kept the chocolates and they'd cost me half a crown.

ॐ ॐ ॐ

A few days later my mum has a bit of good news in the morning post. She gets a letter from the council saying they are going to modernise the house. I'm well pleased for her, she's a great mum, but my dad couldn't care a monkey's about any house improvements; all he's worried about is his shilling pint of Brown and Mild, and a game of crib with his mates at the British Legion. Beer is his life; he works for a brewery in Dagenham and I'm sure his motorbike runs on best bitter. Arthur, my 15-year-old brother, is training to be a chef, God help us. He never washes his hands after going to the toilet, and his middle finger is always up one of his nostrils. He's got acne, and his long finger nails seem to collect the dirt like a hoover. Tonight he's bringing home a bread and butter pudding he's made at college. I'll be giving that a miss. Can you imagine what's in it and what could be floating in the custard? Anyway, I'm out on the pull tonight at the *La Nero* coffee bar in Hornchurch with my mates.

2

Never Trust a Secondhand Car Salesman

Now, my job. I'm called a trainee secondhand car salesman, but it's more like a general dogsbody. The car lot is down the High Road in Seven Kings near Ilford. There are more secondhand car dealers down here than there are Ford Cortinas in Dagenham. On my way to work I put Radio Caroline on and they are playing Dusty Springfield's 'I Only Want To Be With You'. It must take Dusty hours to put her mascara on each morning. On the way in I pass a pick-up point for the local handicapped children, some of them have had polio, and are in a bad way. Poor mites, they haven't got too much to look forward to in life.

On arriving at Tucker's Motor Dealers, I'm greeted by the one and only Eddie Tucker. He's the typical secondhand car dealer, in his mid thirties, swarthy, shifty, dark glasses, gold medallions and wears a crombie. His first comment to me every Monday is,

'Did you get your leg over this weekend?'

And my response is,

'Did you?'

He don't like that because his Mrs caught him out with this blonde petrol pump attendant who worked over the road from us, she was a bit horny. The blonde then moved on to a West Ham footballer and Tucker's Mrs has put him on rations.

The first job of the day is sorting the crud out, or better known as cutting the rust out from the bodywork of one of his latest heaps. You fill the holes in with newspapers, mostly the Sundays as they're a bit thicker. One day he got ratty with me, as I used his favourite *Tit-Bits* magazine to stuff a hole on this old Ford Consul as I'd run out of newspapers. You add a bit of filler and then smooth it off. A bit of spray, and then on to the forecourt for some poor mug to buy.

He gets mostly old bangers so we're always busy. He even does a bit of cut and shut, which to the uninitiated is welding two different motors of the same model together. He'll do anything to get a sale; one poor couple bought this Ford Zephyr off him to go on their honeymoon. It looked a nice motor on the outside, but it had more holes than a colander. The poor bloke paid top whack for it. Eddie being Eddie gave him a bit of the old cockney rhyming slang when it came to the price. The bloke's fiancée took a bit of a shine to our Eddie who played on this. He said to this gullible couple,

'I'll tell you what. It's been a great week for sales, and as you're going on your honeymoon soon, instead of the 500 quid I'm asking for, you can have it for a monkey.'

This bloke hasn't got a clue what Eddie is talking about as he doesn't understand cockney slang. Not wanting to look a prat in front of his bird, he thinks he's being clever in asking Eddie if he can drop the price a bit more. Eddie scratches his head and gets a handful of Brylcreem (as advertised by Denis Compton) for his troubles. After a long, golden silence he says,

'Okay, my final offer is a nut and that's it.'

This bloke thinks he's screwed Eddie to the wall and buys the motor. Eddie does the HP form and gets him to sign it which he's happy to do so, as at £8 a month for five years, he thinks it's a great deal. A few days later, after Eddie has got the clearance from the finance house, the bloke and the girl pick the motor up and everybody is happy. When Eddie gives him a copy of the HP agreement, he accidentally spills his coffee over it. He of course apologises to the punter who's not bothered as he can see his gleaming blue Zephyr, complete with fins, bench seats and column gear stick waiting for him. Eddie adds the finishing touch by giving his fiancée a lovely bunch of flowers. Eddie waves the happy couple off into the High Road and then rubs his hands together.

Now, let's go back to the deal; five hundred quid, of course, is £500. A monkey is slang for £500 and a nut is – wait for it £500 – monkey-nut, which is one and the same. The HP deal is not for five years but ten. When the bloke signed the original form Eddie put his hand over where it said the number of years, because he'd put ten. Also he doesn't put the price of the car on the form, only the breakdown of the monthly payments. By spilling the coffee it smudges that bit so the bloke is unaware it's for ten years. When the five years is up and he finds out he has another five years to pay, he goes to the finance house with all guns blazing. They produce the agreement that shows ten years. By then, Eddie has moved on to another car lot or disappeared. Eddie gets a nice kick-back up front from the finance house for giving them this wonderful bit of business. The punter has no comeback on the motor at any time, as Eddie only guarantees the motor to get you off the forecourt.

𝕩 𝕩 𝕩

I got home from work one night and my mum was in tears. Her mum, my grandma, had died that afternoon. She was a great lady and I was well choked. In the war she helped build Lancaster bombers in Manchester, she gave me a brooch of the plane, which was of perspex from a Lancaster's windshield, made by one of the engineers.

Grandma's house was only just up the road and it had to be cleared out; mum couldn't face doing this as it brought back too many memories for her. So me and Steve said we'd do it for her, as my brother Arthur was useless, and my dad had a bad arm from lifting all those pints.

Grandma had lived in the house for over 60 years; granddad had died five years before. She was a real hoarder, wouldn't get rid of anything so it was a mammoth job; all the valuables were taken back to mum's, including a load of sheet music. My grandma used to play the organ for the silent films at the local picture palace. The rest had to be sorted; every room was jam packed. We started up in the loft which was full of toot, there was a Solent table mangle, a box of powdered eggs, a Vono spring mattress, which was running alive, a box of 1930s Dreft which said 'New Suds Discovery'. There were also two ration books, gas masks, a box of farthings, a wind-up gramophone and a book on the 1953 coronation. There were some model railway engines that my grandfather collected. I took one out of its box; it was a model of that famous engine, *Flying Scotsman*.

We set to work to clear the place out. The rubbish had to be shifted and the tip was six miles away, so we had to find a way of getting rid of it all without wasting petrol. Some 200 yards from grandma's house was a parade of shops. Along the side was a wall that ran the depth of the shops. Twice a day the local road sweeper would put his bag of rubbish there to be collected and a Karrier Bantam dustcart would pick it up. With over 100 bags of grandma's unwanted items, we had to find a way of shifting it. So early each morning, we'd put a few bags up against this wall, and some more in the afternoon. One day we got caught placing it there by the old road sweeper.

'It's you little buggers that are putting all these bags here, then.'

'Sorry mate,' I said.

'I've had a letter from my boss congratulating me on the extra rubbish I'm collecting, and in fact I've been nominated for employee of the month.'

'Well, that's handy then, well done.'

'How much more is there to come?' he said.

'About another 50 bags.'

'I can't live with that son, I'd have to be working 24 hours a day for a month to collect all that.'

I bunged him two bob and said,

'Just close your eyes mate when you put your one bag of rubbish down.'

So we left him talking to himself and went back to collect some more. We were down to the last ten, and it was the day of grandma's funeral. We had to shift these, as the council were coming to re-decorate for the next tenants. So about six in the morning I put them all up against this wall, job done.

Grandma's hearse turned up and the family got into the front car. We had to pass the wall and the bags of grandma's rubbish were still there. As we went by I said out aloud, 'Don't look to the right, grandma,' thinking I was being clever. Of course, my mum looked and saw all these bags; being a woman she put two and two together.

'Nicholas (I hate being called that), please don't tell me that's my mum's worldly possessions up against a brick wall.'

I went very quiet until that little shit Arthur said, with a big grin on his face,

'They are, mum, they are.'

It was best not to say anything, as mum was upset enough. About two weeks later, after she'd forgiven me, the postman came while we were having breakfast. Grandma's post had been re-directed, and mum undid a rather official looking envelope addressed to grandma. She took out the letter and read it.

'No, I don't believe it, how could you Nicholas?'

She threw the letter at me and I started reading it.

> *Dear Mrs Bowers, on the 2nd of this month a number of bags of your refuse were found at the parade of shops at Parkfield. This area is not a place where refuse is allowed to be taken. Within the next two weeks you will be receiving a summons for leaving refuse in an unauthorised place, this could incur a heavy fine or even imprisonment, etc, etc.*

Of course that was the day of the funeral and we must have left her address in one of the bags. Mum left the breakfast table really upset. Arthur was still there.

'You've really cocked up, now,' he said.

'Look, you little shit bag, you say one more word and I'll tell mum where those porno magazines are.'

He left like his bum was on fire. I'd really upset my mum, but she forgave me when I bought her a Frankie Vaughan record.

♪ 3 ♪

Coffee Bars, Mods 'n' Rockers & Brighton

I always looked forward to going to *La Nero* coffee bar with its Italian Gaggia coffee machine, and tonight was no exception. It was a fab place to meet all your mates, and it was our second home. The seats were in blue plastic, and the tables were topped with formica. As I entered, the AMI Continental jukebox was playing the Ronettes number, 'Be My Baby'.

Most of the gang were there when I arrived; Steve, my best mate of course; there was brother and sister Rod and Carol; and Diane who I really had a crush on. She had this lovely perfume on called Intimate. Also there were Anne, Jimmy and Ronnie, a bit of a lad who could get you anything you wanted, and Wendy and Roger who were an item. There was Tony, the drummer with Johnny Brewster and The Tellstars, who were playing tonight, and Alec, who held some great parties. He had a Lambretta TV 175 scooter with loads of extra mirrors, lights, and a bleedin' great fox tail hanging off the back. He was wearing a fishtail parka, with the target sign on the back, which was the Mod icon, and a pork pie hat. He reckoned he was the ace face of the Mods in Essex.

Like all the good things in life there's always cretins who want to spoil it and mess people's lives up. In La Nero that night was the first drug dealer I'd ever come across. The stuff on the scene was mostly Marijuana, Blues, Purple Hearts and Black Bombers. Ted, the guv'nor of *La Nero*, an ex-copper, had a word with him and he was sent packing.

Mind you, sometime later Roger thought he wanted to be a pipe smoker, so on his birthday we'd got him some real top-quality pipe tobacco. We were having a drink down the pub with him to celebrate when he stuffed what he thought was this special tobacco into his briar pipe, instead of his usual Dunhill Mixture. He really was sucking on his old pipe and went through the lot in the one night. He was happy as Larry and bought all the drinks, which was unusual, as he was as tight as a duck's arse. He was off work for two days after that with the biggest hangover he'd ever had. No wonder, it wasn't the drink that caused it, but oodles of marijuana he'd smoked in his old briar. After that he went back to his Golden Virginia roll-ups.

We got our coffees and sat down to listen to the band. The singer Johnny Brewster loved himself; his tight jeans made P.J. Proby's look baggy. His red sequinned shirt and white winkle-pickers told you he was here. Tony, the drummer, was a mate of ours from school. As 11-year-olds, Steve, Tony and me had started up a school band called Tony and the Mustangs. We'd played to lots of local schools and youth clubs. We all wanted to be pop stars, but when me and Steve left school at 15, we turned our attentions to football, while Tony joined Brewster's band. Me and Steve have always kept playing and we'd often have a jam with Tony. We always talked about reforming the band, but never did. I played lead guitar and sang a bit and Steve was on bass. I had a Vivona red and black guitar and a Vox amp.

After he'd set up his drum kit, Tony came over for a chat.

'When are we going to put our own band back together then, Nick? I can't stand working much more with I love Johnny Brewster.'

'You're right, Tony. We did say we'd get back together.'

In one of the breaks when the band stopped playing, the three of us had a long chat about reforming the band. We all agreed we needed a decent singer, and once that person was found we'd go out on the road again and see where it would take us, hopefully to fame and fortune. So now the priority was to find that singer. Our band was starting to take shape, and as we had played together before, we wouldn't be starting from scratch. Give the flash git Brewster his due, he could sing, and his band was superb with 'Tell Me When' by The Applejacks.

The next Bank Holiday weekend me and Steve were off to Brighton in my motor. The rest of our crew were going to Margate. 1964 was the Mods 'n' Rockers era where they all knocked shit out of each other at resort towns, mostly on Bank Holiday weekends. Me and Steve were poor man's Mods, if that makes sense. We couldn't afford the Carnaby Street gear, but we did have the Fred Perry and Ben Sherman shirts, and Sta-Prest trousers. Rockers adopted a biker gang image, wearing black leather jackets, winkle-pickers and tight jeans. Their hair would be swept back with thick sideburns. They would ride motorbikes like a Triumph, Norton, Ariel, Honda or a BSA. Musically they liked Rock 'n' Roll, with the likes of Gene Vincent, Eddie Cochran and Elvis Presley. Mods wore US army type parkas with a furry hood, lightweight designer suits and Fred Perry shirts. They rode Italian scooters, like the Vespa GS160 which had a bulbous back and the Lambretta GT200 with a flat side, or the NSU German Prima D-type. They were easy prey for the Rockers when they met them on the road. Mods generally went for Rhythm 'n' Blues, Soul and Ska music. The Who, The Kinks, Small Faces, and The Yardbirds were some of their favourites. They even had their own magazines called *The Mod* and *The Mods*.

We'd booked up a bed and breakfast just off the seafront for £1 a night, which was a bit expensive, but hopefully it would pay dividends on the crumpet front.

It was chucking it down with rain, the usual Bank Holiday weather, as we left Romford for Brighton on the Friday. The radio went on with the Hollies playing 'Just One Look'. We went through the Blackwall Tunnel and were on our way to Sussex. Halfway to Brighton there was a punch up on the side of the road between a bunch of Mods and Rockers. We passed the scene a bit quick, then Steve shouted out, 'Stop,' which I duly did.

'What's that all about, Steve?'

'Over there look, two birds looking thoroughly fed up.'

The two girls were looking at the mayhem as the Mods and Rockers started to spill blood. One poor Mod was trying to get away from two Rockers, who were swinging a bike chain at him, then this Mod whacked a Rocker with a starting handle, and it was all going off.

I jumped out of the motor first. Steve was a bit better looking than me, and I wanted first pick of these girls. They were soaked through and upset. Fortunately, Steve in his haste to get there first, slipped over and fell, and got a mud pack on his arse. I went up to the girl who looked the tastiest.

'You okay, you look a bit upset?' I said.

'We came with two guys on their scooters and we've had enough, they're always getting into fights.'

The other girl agreed. Steve had now got the mud off his bum and went up to the other girl who wasn't bad, but I was put off by the duffel bag she was carrying, which had printed on it in bold blue letters, 'Metropolitan Police'. It then started to rain harder.

'Do you want a lift to Brighton?' I said to my girl.

'Can we trust you?'

'Of course you can.'

'You haven't got hands of the desert?' the other girl said.

'Of course not.'

They had a quick chat and with the sound of police bells in the background they agreed. They picked up their bags and got into the motor. We'd just left when the police arrived.

Minutes down the road the rain stopped and the sun started to shine. Looking at the two girls in the back, I thought this could be the start of a great weekend. My one's name was Wendy; she was 16 and came from over the river in South London. She was a shorthand typist in Moorgate, in the City. Steve's was called Maureen and she was a receptionist at the same firm. I liked Wendy's bouffant hairstyle, which had the extra height through backcombing. We stopped at the nearest café and while the girls got out of their wet clothes in the toilet, we ordered some bacon sandwiches and four mugs of tea.

The girls came back looking quite delightful. I could see Steve was a bit edgy as he looked at Maureen's bag with 'Metropolitan Police' stamped all over it. Of course, the question had to be asked.

'You sure you're not the Old Bill?'

'Of course I'm not a police officer, Steve, I'm only 16.'

Steve still wasn't happy about the bag as he took a large gulp of tea and a mouthful of bacon sarnie full of Daddies brown sauce. Maureen looked at Wendy and grinned.

'But my dad is, he's a sergeant in South London. He thinks by carrying this bag around with me, it keeps randy blokes like you from trying to get his only daughter's knickers off.'

Well, I've never seen somebody choke on his food like that. Steve went red, and I thought I was going to have to dial three nines. The two girls and I could not stop laughing; I had tears in my eyes. Poor old Steve, there was bacon and tea sprayed up the wall like bullets from a machine gun.

After about five minutes, order was restored and we were ready to move off. In the background we could hear a number of scooters pull up. Wendy glanced out of the window and looked alarmed.

'I think we're going to have a bit of trouble here,' she said to Maureen.

'What's wrong?' I said to Wendy.

'The blokes we came with are outside, and they won't be happy that we're with you two.'

They got up to leave.

'We don't want you two getting involved,' said Wendy, 'You've been really nice to us.'

'Do you want to go to Brighton with them?' I asked.

They both agreed they didn't, and they hadn't even booked the same bed and breakfast as them, which was well handy for us. I, being brave or just stupid said,

'Let's go for it.'

We all walked out into the car park. There were six Mods on their scooters with their parkas on. They looked like they'd been in the ring with Henry Cooper. The Rockers had really given them a right pasting, but unfortunately for us they were still game. Two of the Mods tried to pull the girls away from us but the girls wouldn't move. Me and Steve then got involved. I tried as diplomatically as possible to tell them that they weren't going with them and to leave it out. The one I was talking to was their main man. He had the union jack stamped on the back of his parka. He threw a punch at me which I blocked just in time, and in return I whacked him one on the chin. With that, they all piled into us and for a few seconds I thought it was curtains. Then with the sound of motorbikes in the distance, the Mods stopped fighting. The Rockers came into the car park and surrounded us. It all went quiet and a few arses were twitching, including ours. There were about a dozen Rockers. The main face looked a bit evil, he was a big lump and he came over to us. He stared at me for a few seconds, and then started smiling.

'Hi, Nick! How yah going, mate? Long time no see.'

'I don't believe it, Big Al.'

The Mods were gobsmacked that I knew him. Me and Big Al, as he was known, used to play football for the district team when we were at school. He was a tasty player, and once had a few clubs after him. After a quick chat and exchange of telephone numbers, he made it quite clear that the six Mods with their 'hairdryers', as he called their scooters, were going to be well looked after by him and his mates. We'd have no more trouble with them.

We got in the motor a bit sharpish and made our way to Brighton. The radio went straight on and The Fourmosts' 'A Little Loving' was playing. Love was definitely in the air, and me and Steve couldn't wait to sample some of it.

We dropped the girls off at their B&B and made arrangements to meet them later. We went to our digs. What a khazi we'd picked! The landlady looked like Ena Sharples out of *Coronation Street*; she had the same hairnet on as her and was a right old dragon. She went through all the things we couldn't do in our room.

'No girls, no smoking, no food, no drink, and be back by eleven o'clock, otherwise the front door will be locked. I'm in bed by then and I don't want to be disturbed.'

We thought we were at Colditz. First thing we did was to nick the front door key which was in the lock. Steve went out and got another key cut. Thankfully there were no bolts on the inside of the door, so as long as the key worked we could come and go whenever we wanted. The only good thing about it was that because of a flood in the room that we were supposed to have, she'd put us in two single rooms, which had a connecting door. This was well handy as Steve had really bad smelly feet. It wasn't so much his feet, it was the baseball boots he wore, they had a smell all of their own.

We met the girls that night and had a terrific time at the ballroom. There was a top group called Jimmy King and the Raiders playing. It was an ace night and we danced and drank the evening away. We smooched the last number to a Gerry & The Pacemakers tune, 'Don't Let the Sun Catch You Crying'. We had our goodnight snogs on the sands and made arrangements to see them the next day. We went back to our digs and the front door key we got cut worked well.

The next day after breakfast, which wasn't bad – the only downside was that Ena had this mongrel dog that kept sniffing around you for food – we met the girls on the beach and the sun was shining. We paired off for a couple of hours. Wendy and I moved away as groups of Mods and Rockers were beginning to square up to each other. We went onto the pier to escape the fighting, while Steve disappeared with Maureen. We had a cup of tea and an Eccles cake; I knew how to look after a girl. Afterwards I lit up a Kensitas modern tipped cigarette, as I'd just bought a packet to try out – I went back to the Woodbines. The contraceptive pill had come out in the early sixties, and I wanted to find out whether she was on it. She wasn't and said,

'Don't get any ideas of that nature.'

As we walked back down the pier to meet Steve and Maureen, the Black Marias were out in force scooping up the

Mods and Rockers. One of the Mods had this red and white Vespa, white tyres, extra chrome and a union jack flag hanging on the back. A Rocker was smashing it up with a hammer, and then I saw a couple of Mods do the same thing to his Norton with a metal bar. Another Rocker was kicking the side panels of a Lambretta 150. We were glad to be well out of it.

Wendy was a bit nervous after the trouble they'd had with their blokes the day before. She then let on that they'd been hanging around their B&B, and were getting a bit nasty. They also said to her that they were on the lookout for us in the town, they knew what car we had, and they were going to cause us some damage. The old grey matter was working overtime. We'd already agreed we'd take them back home to South London the following night.

We met up with Steve and Maureen and went to the Ace café for a large fry up. While the girls went to powder their noses, I had a quick word with Steve.

'Right, before they come back.'

'What are you on about, Nick?'

'Just listen, the girls are having a bit of trouble with them blokes they were supposed to come with.'

'How's that?'

'They turned up at their B&B and started to have a pop at them, and they're also looking for you and me to give us a good hiding. My thoughts are that we've got two bedrooms, and as we're gentlemen we can offer them one to sleep in.'

'Sounds the ticket, but how're we going to smuggle them in without Ena finding out. She'd smell a fart in a pigsty?'

'We'll worry about that later. Hang about, the girls are coming back.'

The girls came back nice and refreshed, and there was the smell of Tweed perfume in the air. Wendy looked delightful, with her hipster skirt, which showed her long legs to the full. She had calf-length boots on, and together with her tight tee-shirt showing her ample breasts, she looked well tasty. I couldn't wait for tonight. As we were eating, I knew Steve was still worried about Maureen's Metropolitan Police bag. I felt a wind-up coming on.

'Spoken to your dad over the weekend, Maureen?' I said.

'Funny enough Nick, I spoke to him this morning, he wasn't very happy.'

'Why's that?'

'He's been called out because of the Bank Holiday weekend problems.'

'What, from London?' I said.

'Yeah, he's down on this coast with a few of his PCs from the Met, to help the local police sort out these Mods and Rockers. He might call in and see me.'

Just then a police car with bells ringing went past and Steve nearly shot out of his chair.

We had a great afternoon and we took them back to their digs, Steve looked at me to say you haven't said anything about tonight. We just turned into the girl's road and coming from the direction of their B&B were the six blokes on their scooters. They went by and didn't recognise us. I could see the girls were rattled. I stopped the motor outside their place. Those Mods couldn't have timed it better.

'Look girls,' I said 'I can see them hanging about your digs is causing you grief, so I've got a suggestion.'

'I'm not sharing your bed tonight, Nick, if that's your idea,' said Wendy.

'That's right,' replied Maureen.

'Wendy, have me and Steve tried it on since we first met you?' I replied.

'Well, not really, Nick, except trying to grope my tits and put your hand up my skirt on the beach last night.'

'We'll meet you later for a drink then, if that's okay?'

'Of course it is, Nick. We still want to be with you both, don't we, Maureen?'

Maureen grabbed Steve's hand and said,

'Of course, we're having a great weekend.'

Now, I'm waiting for the hook, as they're getting out of the motor, bingo, we were in.

'By the way what were you going to say to us, Nick?'

'It don't matter, Wendy.'

'No, go on, tell us, Nick.'

'Well, all I was going to say, Wendy, is that we've got two separate bedrooms, I repeat two separate bedrooms, and we was going to offer one of them to you two, and of course me and Steve will share the other room.'

'Oh,' she said.

'I know you're both getting stressed out about these blokes so we thought we'd help you out, but it doesn't matter.'

Wendy looked at Maureen and there was a long silence.

'Yeah, okay, Nick, as long as there's no monkey business.'

'Of course not, Wendy. We'll pick you up about 7.30, then, girls.'

'Oh, by the way, where are those blokes staying, Maureen?' asked Steve.

'Just around the corner at a place called *Sea View*. You're not going to start any trouble with them, Steve, are you?'

'Course not, Maureen, six against two, I don't think so.'

We left the girls and Steve asked me to stop at the local Lipton's. He came back with two bags of sugar. I laughed.

'I don't have sugar in my tea, and by the way, did you get any Green Shield stamps with them?'

Steve looked at me like I was mad and said,

'Let's go round to the guest house and sort those blokes out.'

I knew what he was up to and I drove to their B&B. The six scooters were all nicely lined up outside. We quickly got out of the motor, undid the petrol caps and gave them a good few spoonfuls of Tate and Lyle's finest. They wouldn't be going anywhere on their scooters this weekend. We, of course, wouldn't normally do this to fellow Mods, but self preservation was the name of the game.

In the evening we picked the girls up. They had their bags with them so we went back to our digs to put them into our room. We left the motor outside and walked a few hundred yards to a dance hall called The Shack, where there was a live band playing called Bobby Duke and The Spectors, who were top notch. We had a real great night, with plenty of Whitbread Tankard, and loads of twisting and jiving. The girls had their full quota of Babychams and were well happy. It was a great finish to the night when the Beatles' number 'Twist and Shout' was played. The four of us came out of The Shack at midnight on a high.

❧ ❧ ❧

We make our way back to Colditz, we're all giggling and well soused. As we get near I throw in that we are breaking into our digs, and of course girls aren't allowed in the rooms. They think it's a bit of a laugh and aren't bothered at all. I can see Steve's getting a bit randy, as every few yards he stops to give Maureen mouth to mouth resuscitation. A few yards from Colditz I ask everybody to 'keep the noise down' but what happens, we all burst out laughing. Steve puts the key in the door, gentle like; we're all trying not to laugh. He opens the door slowly, we creep up the stairs and finally reach the top, but then one of Maureen's sling-back shoes falls off and hits every stair loud and clear to the bottom. We hold our breath, will Ena hear it? We're in luck, she doesn't, so Steve goes to retrieve it. Halfway down he falls arse over tit as normal, and joins Maureen's shoe at the bottom. The noise was horrendous; me and Wendy are crying with laughter, and make straight for our room, quickly followed by Maureen. We can hear Ena shouting out in alarm, 'Who's there? Who's there?', and the other residents are opening their doors. Tears are running down our cheeks. Suddenly Steve appears at the door dishevelled, rubbing his leg in pain, and holding Maureen's shoe. All four of us are now paralytic with laughter, but can't make any noise. Then Ena shouts out,

'You naughty popsy, how did you get out, bad boy.'

After a couple of minutes it all goes quiet.

'What happened?' I ask Steve.

'Feckin' winkle-picker caught the metal clip holding her threadbare carpet and the rest is history. You lot were very brave doing a runner, and leaving me there.'

Maureen cuddles up to him and gives him a kiss.

'You can't get around me like that, Maureen,' says Steve. We all burst out laughing again. I have to ask the question.

'How come you didn't get caught?'

'At the bottom of the stairs Ena has this wooden coat stand which I pushed over, I opened the door where her manky dog sleeps and push it out into the hall. I run upstairs, just missing Ena. She sees her popsy next to the coat stand, and of course she thinks the mutt's pushed it over.'

We all look astonished at Steve's story; Maureen looks well impressed, so much so, she grabs Steve's hand and takes him into the other bedroom and closes the door.

'I thought she wasn't like that?' I say to Wendy.

'Well all I say, she doesn't do it much, but when she does, sometimes you hear about it – unfortunately.'

'What do you mean?'

'You'll soon know, Nick.'

'Do you want me to sleep on the floor, Wendy?' I asked.

'What's wrong with the bed?'

I don't need to be asked twice and we both get on the bed, when Maureen shouts out loud from the next room.

'What's that feckin' horrible smell?'

'What's that all about, Nick?' says Wendy.

'Steve's just taken his boots off.'

We both go into one and start giggling. We're having a really great time, when there's a thud, thud, thud coming from the lovebirds next door, as their headboard is making contact with the wall. Every time there's a thud, bits of plaster are coming off our wall, and covering us.

'Oh, no, I thought she'd got over that.'

'What do you mean, Wendy?'

'Well, when she's having sex she can't help herself.'

The noise I can only describe as a screaming banshee, talk about wake the house up, more like the street. Wendy shouts out to her mate to keep the noise down but to no avail. It's no good shouting to Steve, as when he's in full flow there's no stopping him. This goes on and off for ages.

In the morning Steve and Maureen walk into our bedroom like nothing has happened. The first words Steve utter are,

'I'm starving and could eat a horse.'

Looking at Maureen's neck he'd already done it. Me and Steve go downstairs for our full English with all the other residents; this allows the girls to go to the bathroom while nobody is about. When Ena is out of the dining room I nick a couple of bowls of cornflakes and some fresh orange and take it up to the girls. Steve takes the bowls back so Ena won't suss out that we've had girls in the room. Then he goes to the bottom of the stairs to make sure the coast is clear. The girls come down the stairs quickly and go out the front door and into the motor. Me and Steve are just leaving the B&B when Ena appears from the kitchen and comes up to us.

'Had a nice weekend, lads?'

'Brilliant,' I reply.

'Did you enjoy your stay here?'

'Couldn't fault it, your full English was superb.'

'I'm really pleased,' she says.

We're just making a move to go out the front door when she says,

'By the way lads, you owe me two quid for the girls' stay.'

Talk about hearing a penny drop.

'I've had this B&B for over 25 years and I've seen every stroke pulled. You know and I know you've had a couple of girls stay last night, and one of them girls should be in a bird sanctuary; what a racket she makes.'

When she says that, Steve's face is a picture, it's the first time I've ever seen him blush.

'Two quid, lads, or I'll call the police for breaking and entering.'

She pulls out a battered Lloyds Old Holborn tobacco tin, which was full of keys and says,

'Put the key in there.'

'What key?' I say.

'Look, the local bloke who cuts the keys is my neighbour, so he lets me know when my key is being cut.'

'How does he know it's your key?'

'Simple,' she replied, 'my initials are on it.'

Steve takes the key out of his pocket and puts it into the box, then we somehow scrape together two quid in pennies, tanners and some more silver. We hand the money over. We're now completely skint.

'You're lucky,' she says, 'I didn't charge you for their breakfast and the hot water they used.'

'Why do you mess about in locking the door at eleven o'clock?' I ask.

'I wouldn't get my two quids then, would I? Just one thing, the coat stand. Was that you two?'

Both of us just grin at her. We've been done up like a kipper and when we tell the girls they can't stop laughing. The four of us have a final walk along the beach, and it feels like we've known them for years. Hopefully they feel the same, as we've run out of money.

ॐ ॐ ॐ

The Mods and Rockers were having one last punch up on the promenade before going home. We went into a café for some dinner and the girls were great, they put their hands in their pockets and bought us a couple of large portions of sausage toad, chips and beans followed by a Kunzle cake. Wendy went over to the Rock-Ola jukebox and put two tanners in. She picked out 'I Only Want To Be With You' by Dusty Springfield, 'Stay' by The Hollies, 'Sealed With A Kiss' and 'Ginny Come Lately' both by Brian Hyland, 'Don't Let The Sun Catch You Crying' by Gerry & The Pacemakers and 'I Think Of You' by the Merseybeats. Somewhere in all those tunes, there was a message.

We ate our last sausage and listened to the last verse of 'I Think Of You'. It was time to make the journey back to South

London. Wendy and Maureen came good again and gave us some petrol money. We had to wait a few minutes in the café as a big hairy Rocker had just put a Mod through a shop window over the road to us. A police van came out of nowhere and scooped the Rocker up, and flung him in the back, while Sussex Ambulance service took the unconscious Mod to hospital.

The coast was clear and we left the café to go to my motor and home. Suddenly, we came to a stop as a booming voice from behind us shouted out,

'Maureen, stop right there.'

We turned around. Standing there was this big copper built like the proverbial brick shithouse. He was six feet plus, and he was a monster. With him were a couple of young sprog coppers. Maureen said,

'Hello, dad. Still here, then?'

Steve went white, and then red, I thought he was going to collapse. He hastily let go of her hand. Her old man had those piercing eyes that only the Old Bill have. He looked at Steve and then Maureen; you knew what was coming next.

'Had a good weekend, Maureen?'

'Yes, great, dad, just off home now.'

Maureen wanted to move off quickly but her dad stood in her way.

'Where are those six lads from Brixton who promised me personally they would look after you and Wendy?'

'Well, dad, they didn't look after us very well. They were getting into trouble, so we gave them a wide berth.'

So far so good I'm saying to myself, then World War Three kicks in.

'The reason I asked, Maureen, is that we called around to your B&B this morning, early, and you weren't there and the landlady said you never came back last night.'

A nuclear bomb has just gone off and the core of it has just landed on Steve.

'That's right, dad,' she replied. 'Those boys you asked to look after us kept getting into fights. When we got away from them, they kept coming back to the B&B and being nasty to us.'

Maureen was playing a blinder, and then she said,

'These two lads from Essex were our shining knights.'

Forget about the white socks, even in those days Essex was an area that boasted a considerable number of villains, and there's always something about Jack-the-lad Essex boys.

'Essex,' he said. 'You two randy gits are from Essex?'

'Well, yeah,' I replied. 'What's wrong with Essex?'

He looked at his two PCs and said,

'Search them for drugs.'

We both got well frisked and of course they found nothing. Then one of the coppers who was searching Steve said,

'What have we got here, then?'

He pulled out this packet of Johnnies. I thought Maureen's father was going to explode. The copper who'd pulled it out of Steve's pocket, dangled it in front of him. You could see he didn't like his sergeant, as he kept doing it. It was like a pendulum on a clock. The sergeant's eyes kept following it as he was swinging it sideways, which made it even worse. Steve just died and looked up in the sky for God. He wasn't there. Maureen was close to tears, I nearly wet myself from not laughing. Then Wendy stepped forward, and eyeballed Maureen's dad.

'Look, Sergeant Belmont,' she said, 'these lads helped us out, they got alternative digs for us, looked after us, and they're going to take us home. Your Maureen is a good girl; I would've been worried if that packet of Durex wasn't full. I can't believe you'd think that about her. For your information we don't have sex with boys, we're not like that.'

What a performance from Wendy, she kept eyeballing him until he said something.

'Is this true, Maureen?' he said.

With crocodile tears in her eyes she replied,

'Of course it is, dad, what do you think I am, some sort of tart?'

Talk about eat humble pie. He gulped a few times then apologised to the girls and us and gave me a quid for some petrol. Then he got a message from another copper who'd just turned up that the Mods and Rockers had kicked off again, and he had to go. He kissed Maureen goodbye and made us promise that we'd get them home safely. As he went, we all stood there lost for words until Wendy looked at Maureen,

'How'd we get away with that, then?'

While our luck was holding, we hot-footed it back to the motor and made our way to South London. Steve was complaining that the copper had kept his packet of Durex, and to Maureen's utter dismay he said,

'There was only two in there instead of three, you know.'

On the way we got lost and ended up down a country lane. You've got two birds on board and you've got to show off haven't you, and we nearly got killed for it. Me and Steve were feeling a bit peckish and saw some plum trees behind a wall along the road.

'Stop,' he said, 'I feel like doing a bit of scrumping like we used to as kids.'

So I stopped the motor and both of us got out and jumped over the wall. I did point out to Steve that on the brick wall were various signs indicating that this was private property and enter it at your peril.

'But they are lovely looking plums,' said Steve, so he got up the tree and started shaking the bollocks out of a branch.

'Don't make such a racket, there's a house over there,' I said.

Suddenly without warning there was a bang and something flew over our heads. Steve fell out of the tree and landed on the ground, there was another bang.

'It's a bleedin' gun! Somebody is shooting at us,' I said.

We both jumped back over the wall and get in the motor and I drive off like Jack Brabham. We couldn't believe it, but it was true, somebody was having a pop at us over a few poxy plums.

We finally get on the right road to London and put the radio on; Roy Orbison's 'It's Over' was playing. We'd all had a great weekend, except for nearly getting shot. Unfortunately, holiday romances don't always last and normally within a matter of days everybody moves on. Halfway to South London it started to rain big-time, it was lashing it down. Steve shouts out, 'Look at that,' and starts laughing. In front of us was a low-loader lorry with six scooters lined up and strapped down. The Mods whose tanks we'd sugared were huddled together on the back and were getting a real soaking. The girls ducked down so as not to be seen. I slowed down and got by the side of the lorry and sounded my horn, and we gave them the Winston Churchill sign. They didn't look too happy, as they returned the compliment.

We arrived at the girls' houses which were near enough next door to each other. We had our last snogs and took their addresses, as neither was on the phone. After our final kiss, the girls got out of the car, their eyes full of tears. The waves were long and lasting as we disappeared into the distance.

The Sad and Lighter Moments of War

I'd dropped Steve off and finally got home knackered and hungry, but very happy after a great weekend in Brighton. My mum had watched the news on the television regarding the Mods 'n' Rockers, and I had to assure her I wasn't involved. The phone rang and my mum picked it up. (We only had a phone because my dad's company paid for it. He was an engineer, and when there was a breakdown at his firm, they got in touch with him and called him out. We couldn't have afforded a phone ourselves – that was a real luxury.)

'It's for you. It's Tony.' I picked up the phone.

'Hi, mate, how you going, had a good weekend?'

'Nick,' he said, 'We've got an important gig this Saturday, our singer Johnny Brewster's lost his voice, and he's got to rest it for a couple of weeks.'

'Well, why don't you cancel it?' I replied.

'Nick, we really need your help. We want you to sing at the gig.'

'You're joking,' I said, 'I can sing a bit, but I'm not that good, that's why we're looking for somebody to sing in *our* group?'

'This is for a flash guy who lives in Southend. He's got this mansion and has hired a large marquee in his garden for his daughter's 21st birthday party.'

When he told me the road where the bloke lived, I knew they called it Millionaires Row and most of the residents were businessmen or gangsters. Then he told me how much money they were getting for the gig. My share would be £5 which was a lot of money in 1964. I didn't need asking twice, and it was agreed that we'd practise every night for the next week to work out the numbers we were going to play. More importantly, they'd have to work around the numbers I knew.

The gig went out of my head when my dad came home a little bit merry. He'd been to one of his regimental army dinners and was wearing all his medals. I had one of those golden hours with my dad, where there's just the two of us. Mum had popped next door to see one of the neighbours. Arthur had a new girlfriend and he was out with her. I hadn't seen her yet, but one of my mates had seen them out together, and had mentioned something about a lead and a bone, so it didn't sound very promising. Dad went to the little cocktail cabinet and poured himself a large Bells whisky and sat down in his chair. He never normally spoke about the war, but on this one occasion he dropped his guard. He'd been out with his mates and they'd relived a few memories, and he was happy to share one or two with me.

He reckoned he was the first casualty in the war. Ten minutes after war was declared in September 1939, he fell off an army lorry in Chelmsford. He did his back in and stayed in hospital for two weeks. He was a sergeant in the Royal Artillery and was stationed out in Burma fighting the Japanese. He was in communications and led about 40 men. He wouldn't go into some of the atrocities he witnessed, but with tears in his eyes he did tell me that his best mate, Bert from East Ham, was blown up in front of him. All that was left of him was a foot in one of his army boots. He'd known Bert since they were kids and they'd done everything together. They were like brothers and he still thought about him everyday. He went to the cabinet and refilled his glass. While he was doing this I thought about me and Steve who were like brothers. I'd known Steve ever since we could walk and couldn't imagine seeing my best mate blown to bits in front of me. I shivered at the thought of it. My dad sat down again and I didn't push him anymore. He then said he recalled one funny story in Burma when they were deep in the jungle and were running out of food. Some supplies were parachuted in, which included a live goat. The goat was their fresh meat. My dad started smiling to himself and said,

'All my men were armed to the teeth with all types of weapons including machine guns and an assortment of knives. But not one of the men had the heart to kill the goat and they let it run off.'

On another occasion there were about ten of them going through a Burmese village on a mission, when suddenly one of the villagers pulled them into his hut and put his hand over his mouth motioning for them to keep quiet. They were all given a cup of whisky and a cigarette. Then he indicated again for them to keep quiet. Within a few seconds a number of Japanese soldiers walked past the hut where they were, and disappeared into the distance. My dad said,

'It was an unreal situation smoking a cigarette and enjoying a whisky while the enemy walked by within a few feet of you.' He always wondered where they'd got the whisky from.

Every night for the next week, except Friday when I was going out with Steve, I met up with the guys from The Tellstars and we worked out some sets that we felt comfortable with for the coming gig at the mansion in Southend. I had a chat with Tony about the start of our band; the right singer hadn't been found yet, but we were working on it.

After practice on the Thursday night I had a quick drink with Rod and Carol, they were great friends of mine and came from a lovely family. Rod was one of those good-looking blokes, and nice with it. He worked in the building trade. He also played in the same football team as me and Steve. I had a crush on his sister, Carol; she really was a smashing girl and worked for a travel agent. I did try and date her a few times. In fact we did go out to the pictures one night, but she was really only interested in the film, which was *Zulu*. Two of the actors were Stanley Baker and Jack Hawkins. It didn't help when a mouthy usherette called Doreen opened her gob. She went to the same school as me and was a ringer for the female equivalent of Billy Bunter. She shone her torch on two seats at the back row and said in a snide way,

'These are the two seats you usually take them to, for your snogging.'

Carol did kiss me goodnight, but she made it quite clear in the nicest possible way that I was a bit too brash for her. I thought brash was a nice word, she probably meant gobby. Anyway we were great mates, and we used to speak to each other most weeks, or see each other when the gang met up.

♫ 5 ♫

———•••———

Birdin' It

On Friday nights we used to go birdin' it down the local High
Street, as we used to call it. Friday was *Ready, Steady Go* night
on the television; you'd always watch that before you went
out. That pop music programme was first broadcast in 1963,
and it was our God to music. The signature tune for this
show was introduced by The Surfaris' record 'Wipe Out' and
later Manfred Mann's '5-4-3-2-1'. They had a competition
to find the next Beatles, called Ready, Steady Win. This was
won by The Bo Street Runners. The main presenters were
Keith Fordyce and Cathy McGowan. The last ever show was
in December 1966. I liked *Ready, Steady Go* a lot better than
Juke Box Jury with David Jacobs.

In the sixties you could drive along any High Street in
England looking for girls to take out for a drink. It went
like this. You're in your motor and you'd see a couple of girls
walking in the distance. Steve would say, 'Thirty yards on the
left.' I'd stop the car and Steve would wind down the window
and say something corny like, 'It's a bit cold out there, girls'
or, straight to the point, 'Would you like to go for a drink?'
If and when the girls got in the motor with us, they were
safe. If after a short time they didn't fancy us we would of
course drop them off home. All we wanted was some fun and
hopefully so did the girls. Once the girls were in the motor
and everybody seemed happy we'd take them to a pub. Lager
was being introduced more and more, and most girls wanted
a lager and lime, which was the in drink. Unfortunately, it was

a bit expensive so we got them a cold light ale with lime. Most of them didn't know the difference, so it wasn't a problem. After a couple of drinks and if we got on well with them, we would take them home via a little spot for a snog. This place where we parked was under some trees, just off the main road. The track was only 20 yards long and the trees covered it well. One night we were in my motor, enjoying ourselves with a couple of girls. Without warning there was a tap on the window, talk about crap ourselves! I thought it might have been the Old Bill. I gingerly opened the misted window and there standing in front of me was an old boy, carrying a crook, with his trusty dog, he looked like a farmer.

'Look lads,' he said, 'I've noticed your car here a few times and this is my property.'

'Sorry about that guv,' I replied.

'I'll tell you what, lads, I don't want to spoil your fun, so every time you come here I'm going to leave a tray of eggs under this bush,' which he pointed out. 'You take the eggs and you put two bob in the tin which will be next to the eggs and everybody is happy.'

We couldn't believe it. Talk about going to work on an egg! Mum did comment, when I took them home,

'There's no little Lion stamped on those eggs.' She was a bit worried about that.

This went on for about a year. We never saw him again, but the eggs were always there.

Sometimes we'd have a chat over a pint, and discuss the week's talent. After the end of one week we did have a laugh about the birds we'd pulled. One girl called Mary had this liberty bodice on, which was a thick, fleecy, fabric vest with rubber buttons, which I gather you wore when you were a kid. It was impossible to shift. I asked her why she had it on.

Clearly looking embarrassed, she said,

'My mother made it quite clear that I couldn't go out tonight without this on, as there was boys out there who would try and take advantage of me.'

Her mum was spot on, and there was no answer to it, there's no way I could take a 'liberty' with her.

Steve had fallen for this girl called Vicky, but I didn't fancy her mate. He'd met her a couple of times, and was starting to fall in love as you do, so I had to put a stop to it. I mentioned to him that I'd spoken to Rod who knew Vicky. I pointed out to him that he'd told me she had a real bad case of pyorrhoea. I said to Steve,

'I've checked it out in my mother's family medical health book and the term pyorrhoea means a discharge of pus from the sockets of the teeth that can cause chronic infection and ulceration of the gum margins, which extend into the tooth-sockets. It also can destroy the lining of the teeth.'

Steve had just left Vicky an hour ago and started spitting to try to clean his mouth out, and then he looked down below! He immediately jacked her in. He wasn't happy with me later when he found out that Rod didn't know her, and what I'd said was a load of lies.

Friday nights locally were not good for pulling girls. Many used to go to an American airbase where there was always a dance with great live bands. The soldiers had a field day and they must have thought it was Christmas every Friday night. Coaches were laid on for the girls to take them to the camp. They were known affectionately as 'the meat wagons'. We did try to go to Victor Silvester's dance night on a Friday at a local hall to learn ballroom dancing. We thought we'd meet a classier bird. Unfortunately, we weren't the type of person they wanted there, so we were booted out on our first night.

One night we were in deepest Suffolk. We'd met two girls at a dance and were taking them home to the village where they lived. Steve was driving a big old Humber Hawk which he'd borrowed from work unofficially. The bloke had dropped it off to have four new tyres fitted, so Steve was test driving it for him. It was quite a foggy night and the village was on the edge of nowhere. As you do, you stop for a goodnight kiss. We were at this remote place with a clump of trees and a bit of open ground. With Steve driving he made it quite clear that he was staying in the motor, and me and my bird were going outside.

I really didn't fancy going out in the dark, as you couldn't see anything and it was foggy. But the things you do for a snog. Me and my girl walk out into the wilderness, while jammy Steve was in the warm listening to Radio Caroline and enjoying his goodnight grope. I was leading this girl to I don't know where and found a big oak tree in the middle of nowhere and we started enjoying each other's company. The fog was now lifting, and we were up against this tree making a bit of a noise. Without warning there was a hoot above us, which sounded like an owl, and a dead mouse with blood oozing out of its mouth dropped at our feet. As the fog lifted we saw the eerie ruins of what seemed to be a castle. That was too much for me and the girl. She was screaming,

'Get me out of here, get me out of here.'

I was scared myself as well, so we legged it back to the motor. Steve and his girl heard the commotion and got out of the car as we arrived back. My girl was crying and Steve said later my hair was standing on end.

After it had all calmed down Steve put his headlights on; there was a sign on a wall pointing to the Norman castle ruins. Our night was also in ruins, but as we drove them home we were all laughing our heads off within a few minutes.

♪ 6 ♪

Posh Gig

It was the day of the 21st birthday party and I was to be the lead singer with the band, because Johnny Brewster was sick. Steve turned up about six o'clock, awash with Old Spice; he was coming to the gig with us. A few minutes later a big old Bedford van pulled up outside the house and there's a loud beep on the horn, the band was here. I jumped in the van with Steve. Tony and the boys took the piss out of my checked flares, and Tony said that if I put some bells on the bottom of my trousers I'd look like Noddy. The boys were a good bunch, and in one way they were happy that Johnny Brewster wasn't going to be there tonight, as it gave them a better chance of pulling a bird. Normally, the best looking girls went for the singer first. We pulled into the drive of the mansion. Parked in the car park were Rollers, Mercedes, Mini Coopers and various other high-class motors. We pulled up alongside this new Jag and got out of the Bedford. He must have been waiting for us, because the bloke who owned the mansion came up to us. He was a bit posh, but seemed okay. Tony went over to him and took him to one side for a chat. He came back a few minutes later and gave us the SP.

'Right,' he said, 'This bloke seems a toff, he's already given me the money for the gig up front.'

'He hasn't heard us play yet,' I said.

'No, but his daughter Andrea, whose birthday it is, has, and that's good enough for him.'

'But that was with the Brewster singing, not me,' I replied.

The bass guitarist Robin, who was smoking this evil-smelling roll up of Old Shag, laughed and said,

'That's alright, Nick, lose my gig money tonight because you can't sing and you'll be walking home.'

Tony got a couple of the lads to drive the Bedford round to the back of the house to unload the gear. In the garden was the biggest marquee I'd ever seen. It looked about the size of a football pitch. We walked in and what greeted us was out of this world. There's the fanciest bunting you could imagine, wishing Andrea a Happy 21st Birthday, different class, especially the bar, which was massive, with every type of drink you could imagine. The hot and cold food was being prepared, and it looked fit for a king. I asked a guy with a dicky bow on, how many people were expected.

'Around 300 plus,' he replied.

The band looked at each other. They normally played to about 50 to 100 people.

'Right lads,' Tony said, 'we've got about an hour before we're on stage, so we need to get moving.'

We all got busy plugging in and did a soundcheck, till we were happy. We were going to do three sets, and all the numbers were written out for each band member. Steve had disappeared while we'd been doing this. He finally turned up with a light ale in his hand, and a quite delightful young lady by the name of Petra, who looked a bit naughty. He introduced us to her and he was full of it. He knew he'd pulled a real stunner and he was going to enjoy himself all night. When she went to the bar, Steve was showing off.

'Did you smell that horny perfume she had on, it's called 'In Love', by Hartnell.'

We were all well impressed with his knowledge of the scent industry. Petra was Andrea's best friend and when she returned from the bar, she had a message from Mr. Goldstein, the owner of the house. We could drink what we wanted within reason, and food was laid on for us and would be brought over at each of the breaks. We went over to the bar to bring back a few drinks. They had Younger's Tartan on, which was handsome, and also on the table was a box of Romeo y Julieta cigars. I helped myself to a couple – made a change from a Woodbine.

We were doing the last soundcheck and the place was bursting. All the men wore dicky bows and the women looked stunning in expensive outfits. I looked at my checked flares, union jack tee-shirt and baseball boots. I looked like a bag of shit, but I was a rock star, so it didn't matter. Or was I? We'd soon know.

Mr. Goldstein came over and asked me to hand the microphone to him, which I duly did. He asked us, when he'd finished speaking to the guests, to play Happy Birthday to welcome his daughter into her party. The lights went low and a spotlight was shone on Andrea as she walked in. She had this stunning dress on, which was upmarket, probably bought from Biba in London. It certainly wasn't from Romford Market where I got my toot from. She wasn't a stunner but she had class stamped all over her. She was followed in by a bloke a bit younger than her; he looked smart as well. Andrea gave a twirl to everybody and sat down at a table close to us. She looked over to me to say you can start. I looked at the band and we were ready to ride. We started with a Swinging Blue Jeans number called 'The Hippy Hippy Shake' which normally gets them in the mood, followed by a Brian Poole & The Tremeloes number, 'Do You Love Me'. The first chord had been struck and we were in business. The first set went down well and everybody seemed happy. We got a drink from the bar and some posh nosh was brought over to us, which was well tasty. It was the first time I'd ever tasted beef goulash, and I finished it off with pineapple upside-down cake and a sherry trifle. Steve had a starter, which was potted shrimps, followed by coq au vin and his sweet was a soufflé. It was better than the fish and chips we usually had on a Saturday night. Andrea came over to me, followed by her boyfriend.

'You're not the same singer I met at a coffee bar in Ilford?' she said. 'What's your name?'

'Nick.'

'What's happened to the usual singer, Nick?'

'He's lost his voice, I was a last minute replacement.'

'I'm really pleased with the band, and I like your voice.'

It was just as well as she said her father was going to try and book a local band, The Paramounts, who had that great record 'Poison Ivy'. Tony shouted out that it was time for the second set.

'Nick,' she said, 'Would it be possible for me to sing a song tonight? I've sung quite a lot before.'

I was taken aback, but she was the birthday girl.

'That won't be a problem, as long as the band knows the number.'

'The Gerry and the Pacemakers' song 'You'll Never Walk Alone,'' she replied.

'Come back at the end of the second set, Andrea, and we'll sort it out.'

Tony shouted out, '1,2,3', and we went into The Beatles' 'Can't Buy Me Love'. We finished the second set with The Searchers' song 'Needles and Pins'. Everyone had been up dancing and that was a good sign they were enjoying themselves. When we finished, I had a quick word with the band, and there wasn't a problem with the number that

Andrea wanted to sing, they knew it, and she appeared to have a bit of singing experience.

As Robin said with a laugh, 'The money they're paying us tonight, I'd even play the Bernard Cribbins number, 'Right Said Fred'.'

Andrea came back and was well pleased when I said she could sing the last number.

'What key do want to sing in, Andrea?'

She gave me a puzzled look and said,

'What's a key?'

The bells started ringing, I should've known then. She introduced me to her boyfriend Rick and moved off quickly to tell her dad the good news about her singing. Rick seemed a nice guy and he certainly wasn't posh. I shook his hand.

'Don't blame me, will you,' he said.

He went to the bar and bought me back a large brandy.

'You're going to need this.'

He walked away grinning to himself. While I'd been talking to Andrea, all the boys in the band had sorted out a nice array of girls for later. It's a fact of life, girls do like blokes in bands, until they're out every night playing, or on tour somewhere. Then the novelty wears off, especially when the band members are shagging anything that moves, getting drunk and popping a few pills.

We began the last set with the Beatles' song, 'Love Me Do'. When it was the last number, I called Andrea over on the microphone to come and join us. Everybody stopped, clapped and cheered as she made her way to the stage. I gave her the full intro bit and handed her the band's new Shure microphone, which she dropped. I picked it up and handed it back to her; fortunately it was still working. She then turned around to the band and said, 'Let's go boys.'

The band started to play and she started to sing 'You'll Never Walk Alone.' It was feckin' horrendous, it brought back memories of the screaming banshee in Steve's bedroom at Brighton. If she sings like this again she'll always be alone, I thought. The guests went very quiet and I've never seen so many people go to the bog at the same time. Then some clown in the crowd started shouting out, 'More, more'. He must have been an Everton supporter, the tune being the Liverpool football club anthem. What do I do?, I'm saying to myself. The girl is dying on stage on her 21st birthday, she's only sung for about 20 seconds and she's cleared the hall out. I've got to go and sing with her and help her out.

Then Rick, her boyfriend came on to the stage, and went up to one of the group's Reslo microphones and started singing with her. This boy could sing, he saved the night. By the end of the number everyone had come out of the bog and was cheering madly for more, which they weren't going to get. The number finished, and after Andrea had done about ten bows to the cheering crowd, she walked off the stage. The saddest thing of all is that she thought she was the next Lulu, but our band wasn't going to be her Luvvers. With the last number sung, the balloons came down in their hundreds and then the fireworks started to go off outside. As everyone rushed to see the spectacle I got hold of Rick's phone number. We'd found our singer.

The next day after speaking to Tony and Steve, we all agreed that we wanted him to join the band, so that night I gave Rick a bell, but I didn't tell him what it was all about.

On the Monday I met Rick at a pub in Brentwood where he lived. I bought him a drink and we sat down.

'Sorry about Andrea's singing, or lack of it,' he said, 'she's dire.'

'I did notice, but that's not why I wanted to have a chat.'

'What's it all about then, Nick?'

'I'll get straight to the point. Tony out of the Tellstars, Steve and me, thought your singing was ace at the party.'

'Is Steve the guy who was with Petra?'

'Yeah, why?'

'Well, you tell him to keep away from her, unless he wants crabs, she's got more on her than Southend beach, I should know I'm still itching.'

We both fell about laughing. Isn't it funny that when somebody says something like that, you automatically start scratching.

'We are forming a band and we want you to be the singer.'

'You're joking?'

'No, we're well serious Rick, we want you on board.'

'I've never sung in a band before.'

'Where did you learn to sing like that, then?'

'You won't laugh, Nick.'

'Try me.'

'I used to have singing lessons when I was a kid, and I was in the school and church choirs. Then I did a bit in a local amateur dramatic society, but then I discovered sex at 13, and packed up being a thespian.'

'You can sing all right, Rick, and I know all of us would get on well, we'd have a great laugh.'

'One problem, Nick.'

'What's that?'

'Andrea. We're planning to get engaged soon and she wouldn't be happy with me being in a band. She's one of those birds who wants you all to herself.'

'That's a real pity, Rick; would you think about it and give me a ring?'

'Sure, I'll do that.' It was left that he was going to ring me.

Next day I had a drink with Tony and Steve at our local, *The Queens Arms*. I explained that I'd met up with Rick and he was going to let us know if he was going to join the band. While we were enjoying a pint of Forest Brown, I noticed Steve was scratching his nuts vigorously.

'By the way Steve, did you have a good night with Petra?'

'Great, what a raver, she couldn't get enough of it all night.' He started scratching again.

'Rick said she's got more crabs on her than Southend beach.'

'No, you're not going to get me with that old chestnut, I still remember that lovely girl Vicky, who you said had pyorrhoea.'

He started to scratch again. About 20 minutes later the seafood man came into the pub with his basket of fresh fish to sell. I bought some winkles for my dad, he did love a winkle, and he was an expert with the pin pulling them out of the shell. In the basket as well was this big ugly crab that was on the move.

'Where'd you get your crabs from mate?' I asked.

'Southend,' he replied, 'You get a nice crab down there.'

Steve pulled a face and disappeared into the bog to check he hadn't got the Southend itch.

I later found out from Rick that it was one big giant wind up about Petra. Her surname was Crabbe, and she lived near Southend.

♪ 7 ♪

Football

Football was a big part of our lives. I played Senior Amateur football with Steve and Rod, which was a good standard. The senior team meant you got paid unofficially, or boot money, as it was called. The league we played in was the Athenian League, the clubs were mostly London based or from the South of England. Our club was called Haynham Town. I remember playing against Eastbourne FC at The Saffron's, which was like a park pitch; it had a rope around the ground for the supporters to stand behind. Eastbourne is renowned for its elderly residents, but they were rascals. I was running with the ball and was near the rope, when a couple of the old boys poked their walking sticks out and tried to trip me up.

I played left back at Haynham Town. We were a middle of the road team and were paid £1 a week, not in cash, but with a draw ticket for the social club raffle. I remember one game where I had a blinder and got man of the match. After the game I was presented with a poxy turkey, the first prize in the raffle. We played in the FA Cup and FA Amateur Cup. We were drawn against a team from West London one time in the FA Cup 1st qualifying round. We knew we were in for a war and made sure for our game against them that we had our long shin pads on; I had the ones which had canes imbedded in them. We all got changed and the manager explained our tactics of how we were going to play them, which wasn't much, as all he said was,

'It's everyman for himself out there.'

This didn't give us much to look forward to for the next 90 minutes. To be fair we were blessed with some hard players and I was no shrinking violet. They had a centre forward nicknamed Billy the brain surgeon, because he was brainless. He was built like a tank and was the original animal. If they kicked off first, they'd hold on to the ball, while Billy ran as fast as he could towards our goalkeeper. They would then pass it back to their centre half who'd hit a long ball towards our keeper, who would come out and try and collect it. As he did so, Billy would try and get the ball and in doing so would take the goalkeeper out. This had happened to us when we played them the previous year and Billy put our young goalkeeper in hospital, so we were ready for him.

They won the toss and kicked off to start the match. It all went to plan and Billy ran towards our goalkeeper. Our goalie came out to get the ball, and as Billy was going to do his dirty deed, our six-foot-plus centre half Kenny timed his tackle perfectly and went through him like a knife through butter. The brain surgeon lost it and tried to spank Kenny, who just laughed at him. The referee sent Billy off, and after that, their team lost it and we beat them easily, 3-0.

Our right winger Andy loved himself. He would get out of the bath after the game and put all this smelly stuff all over himself. One day one of the lads put itching powder in his tin of Avon. Andy came out of the bath, got the old talcum powder, lifted his tackle up and gave it a good helping underneath. Then he talced himself all over. It only took a minute to kick in before he was running up and down the pitch scratching his goolies off, and shouting retribution to the idiot who'd done this to him.

There was another player, Danny who had this dirty old jock strap he used to wear. It was horrible and we were sure there were things living on it. So one day before a game we greased it up with Whitfield's, which is an ointment to treat soreness in the cracks at the top of your legs which we called jock strap rash. This stuff is dynamite and when it hits the spot you get this burning sensation that makes you feel like you're on fire. If you get it on your nuts it's agony. Danny put his jock strap on; as the Whitfield's touched his skin, he jumped up like someone had shoved a red hot poker up his bum. He ran like a lunatic into the communal bath and ripped his jock strap off. He then stuck the cold water tap on and let it run all over his nuts to get rid of the burning. He never wore that again.

I also played a season for Bentfield Town whose first team were semi-professional players in the Southern League. I played for the reserve team which was all kids and a few professionals. The reserves were affectionately known as the stiffs. The Metropolitan League was also a good standard of football playing against the likes of West Ham's third team and Wimbledon, which was my first game for them. I was only 15 and we played at their Plough Lane ground. We lost 2-1 and there was well over a thousand people watching. At the end of the game lots of kids ran onto the pitch for autographs. They all went past me, so I stopped one young boy.

'Do you want my autograph?' I said.

'You must be joking mate; I want a proper footballer, not a wanker like you.'

On another occasion we were getting walloped by Bury St Edmunds 6-0, and a wag from the crowd shouts, 'Play for a draw, Bentfield.' There were only two minutes to go.

There was another real laugh. We had a match on the Kent coast. It was a filthy day, raining cats and dogs. The pitch was a mud bath with deep puddles everywhere, in fact they found a cod in the centre circle! Their goalkeeper was a bit of a veteran, but could still play a bit. It was about even in the first half. The second half we came good and went into a 2-0 lead. Then with only about ten minutes to go we were awarded a penalty. Mick, our inside right, was our ace penalty taker. To the right of the keeper was a large puddle. Mick hit the penalty hard and true, but the goalie pulled off a magnificent save. That was the good news. The ball went one way and the keeper's wig went the other, and landed in the puddle. For a few seconds none of us realised what had happened, until we saw this floating rug. Mick could have followed up and put the ball into the net, but with the ball going one way and the wig going the other, he didn't know which one to kick first. We all creased up and it took a bit of time to re-start the game. The poor keeper was as bald as a coot, and there he was, fishing his wig out of the puddle. He tried to put it back on but it was having none of it. Even his own team mates didn't know he had this hair-piece, as this was his first game for the club. We did have a beer with him later and he took the ribbing well.

Moving forward a bit, I was involved in one of the funniest stories in football that I can remember. It happened when I played one game for another senior football team on the outskirts of Essex in 1965. I only played one game for them, because as you will see, I was doing something else, which never allowed me much time to play football. Both their fullbacks were injured, and the captain Alan, was asked by the manager if he knew anybody who could help out for the game. Alan was a good mate and asked me if I could play. The manager was on another planet when it came to training. Picture this; it's snowing so hard you can't see in front of you. We couldn't go on to the pitch because of the snow, so what does he do? He has us running in the car park in-between all the motors for two hours. Does that make sense? I thought what have I joined here? After this training session, the manager was taken to one side by the chairman, and given the sack because of a run of bad results. The chairman then talked to the players.

'The manager has left, but not to worry, we've a new manager in place for Saturday's important game at Uxbridge.'

'Who is it?' said the club captain Alan, to the chairman.

'Ronald Taplow-Watts,' he replied.

All the players looked at each other to say, 'Who the hell's he?' Another player called Harry said,

'I've heard of him, he runs a Sunday morning side in division five in the local league, he knows nothing about football.'

The chairman did a body swerve and just said,

'Be at the ground at 11.30 for the game at Uxbridge.'

৯ ৯ ৯

On the Saturday morning we duly turn up at the ground to catch the coach, which looks pre-war. Anyone who's played senior football knows that when you go to an away match you want to travel in a half-decent vehicle, it just gives you that edge. The new manager is an old boy of about 40 and he's standing by this heap of crap. He's wearing a tracksuit that is far too tight, and his Double Diamond beer gut is hanging over it. I'm a young sprog and normally I give an opinion on anything, but sometimes you know when to keep your gob shut, and this was one such time. He herds us into this cattle truck and we all sit down. He stands in front and makes it quite clear he's the manager and wants to be called Boss. One of the players shouts out,

'Boss, does that mean you aren't the manager of that great Sunday morning side, Lea Rovers Old Boys reserves, who are holding up the bottom of league five, anymore?'

Everyone in the coach starts laughing and he doesn't know where to put himself. We're all waiting for the driver to show, as we've got to go across London, which will take a bit of time. Then to everybody's amazement, the boss gets into the driver's seat. He puts the coach microphone in the stand on the dashboard and switches it on. Then he comes over loud and clear, '1,2,3, testing' which he says three times. He switches the engine on and a cloud of toxic smoke covers the whole car park. Then he reverses into a metal dustbin which sounds like a bomb going off. He finally gets us into the High Street, and we're off to play Uxbridge in an important Division One clash. I bet the likes of George Best, Jimmy Greaves and Dave Mackay don't travel like this, I'm saying to myself.

You've got to imagine it. He's driving through the heart of London on a Saturday, with Tottenham and West Ham playing at home. Because of this, we get caught in every traffic jam possible. This coach is rattling your bones, and springs are non-existent. Your nuts are jumping about like a couple of ferrets in a slipper, and you're holding on to the metal handrail in front of your seat for dear life. Then we hear, 'Testing, 1,2,3' and the boss is at it again. One of the boys shouts out,

'What's your name, bleedin' Len Barry?' (Remember that record?)

Then, while driving the coach, he starts giving us a running commentary on how we're going to play, what our tactics are going to be, and who's taking corners and free kicks. It would be hard enough just to drive it, let alone talk over a microphone, and look at notes stuck on the steering wheel. I've never seen a whole coach of people look at each other in utter amazement. He's in and out of the traffic, how we never hit something I'll never know.

The chairman, who's travelling with the other committee men, disappears under his seat, never to be seen again. The captain, Alan, is a black cab driver and as we get nearer to the ground, Alan stands up and shouts out,

'Boss, I need to tell you something.'

The boss ignores him and goes back into his drivel over the microphone.

'Boss, I need to tell you something now,' said Alan.

'Tell me when we reach the ground,' the boss replies.

'But boss, I need to tell you right now.'

The coach finally gets to the ground and enters the car park in a cloud of smoke and comes to a standstill. The boss switches the engine off and it's heaven. For the last three hours we've had to listen to Lord Haw Haw and the noise of a Sherman tank. Then one of the funniest things I've ever heard in football. Alan majestically rises from his seat, looks around at everybody in the coach for an audience.

'Boss, who are we playing today?'

'Well, what a stupid question from our club captain? Uxbridge Town of course, who'd you think we're playing.'

'So why have you brought us to Ruislip Manor's ground, then?'

I'd thought it was a bit funny that there was another coach in the car park with a headboard for Croydon FC on it, who of course were playing Ruislip Manor. The team erupts in laughter and tears are running down our faces. Then panic sets in as the boss swings the coach out of the car park and goes like a bat out of hell to get to Uxbridge Town's ground in record time.

We arrived just about 10 minutes before kick-off, and if I recall we got a draw out of the game. The boss only lasted four games with the club. I wonder why?

♪ 8 ♪

The New Singer

Eventually I got a phone call from Rick, who we'd met at the birthday party. I was expecting bad news, but no, he was up for it and wanted to be the singer of our new group, great news. I arranged to ring him back later so we could all meet up. I contacted Tony and Steve and they were well pleased. It was the second bit of good news I'd had that week. Me and Steve had put a bet on a horse called 'Santa Claus' that was running in the Derby. We were a bit worried because the jockey, Scobie Breasley, had had 12 attempts at winning this race without success. But it was lucky 13 and we'd earned ourselves a nice few quid which set us up for the week.

I'd already found a place for the band to practise. My mum was the cleaner for the local vicar, and the old boy said we could use the church hall whenever we wanted. It was handy as the football season had finished and pre-season training wasn't for another two months, so I could just concentrate on the band. After a few phone calls we agreed to meet up at the hall on the Thursday night for the first session. Me and Steve kept the Friday night free as that was the night we went birdin' it and to top ourselves up with eggs!

I was at work on the Wednesday and was cleaning this nice silver, two-door, deluxe Ford Cortina 1200. Why I say it was a nice motor is that it didn't have any rust and it wasn't a ringer. Eddie was fannyin' around me like an old woman, making sure I hadn't missed anything. I knew it was for a special punter as he filled it up with a tank full of petrol, and that wasn't like him. About half-hour later this Jag pulled up outside the car lot, and Eddie looked a worried man. I didn't take too much notice at first until I saw two well-known Essex villains and one of their henchmen getting out of the motor. As they made their way over to us, one of them said to me, 'Hello, boy,' and they both disappeared into the portakabin with Eddie. The henchman, who I'll call Mr. Smith, stayed with me. He had a good look around the motor and seemed impressed.

'This isn't a rust bucket or a cut and shut, son?' he said.

'No, the motor is ace and it runs like a dream,' I replied.

'Will it get me away from a bank quickly?' he said with a laugh.

He sees me pull a face and says,

'Only joking son.'

Or was he? About two months previously I had to pick up a Ford Capri from an Irishman in a pub car park in Kilburn, North London. I drove it back to the car lot and it was put on the front. About a week later the Old Bill were crawling all over it. They informed Eddie that it had been used in a bank robbery in Buckinghamshire.

A few minutes later the two villains came out of the portakabin, got into their Jag and sped off, while Mr. Smith drove the Cortina away. Eddie came out sweating profusely, lit a Capstan full strength and inhaled deeply. He then took a gulp of brandy from a hip flask.

'How much did you get for it then, Eddie?'

Eddie starts coughing his lungs up.

'Money,' he said ,'money, you don't get money off them, you give it to them, and I've got to find them another motor as well.'

'How come you're in debt to them?'

'My brother Sam went away for a five-year stretch and while he was gone, his Mrs and kids got a bit of a pension each week off them, and so in return they expect a favour from me.'

'You told me your brother got out of prison three months ago, why can't he return the favour?'

'Because he's disappeared off the face of the earth to get away from them, so they collect from me instead.'

The following week when Eddie acquired this other motor, which was a Morris 1100, I had to deliver it to a heavy-duty bloke known as Mr. Brown, a very close associate of these villains. He lived in a large house with a massive drive. I drove in and there was a number of menacing looking German Shepherds roaming about. Out came Mr. Brown with muscles bulging. He told the dogs to shut up which they did, they were as frightened of him as I was. He took me into his house and offered me a cup of tea. As he closed the front door I looked up and saw a sawn-off shotgun above the door, held on by two clips. We walked into his kitchen and his Mrs made me a cup of tea. Then he asked the same old question,

'This motor is a good'un, isn't it, because it's for my daughter, and I wouldn't like it to be a wrong'un, if you get my meaning?'

I gave him the assurance that he wanted, but I was worried, because this motor once belonged to a bloke who'd hammered it a bit. I'd had my tea, so how was I going to get back to Seven Kings? Mr. Brown stood up and said,

'I'll drop you off at the station, I've got to see a mate nearby.'

He got into the 1100 and said,

'I'll give it a test run to make sure it's okay.'

As we got into the motor I had my fingers crossed. We sped off and he was doing his Jim Clark bit. We arrived at the station in no time at all; fortunately the motor behaved itself. As I was getting out he gave me a quid and said,

'Tell Eddie if there's any trouble with this motor I'll be around to see him with my friend Mr. G,' and with that he sped off.

As I was sitting in the train I was wondering who Mr. G was? The penny did drop later when I spoke to Eddie.

'Mr. G is his pet name for his gun,' he said.

I looked at Eddie and for a minute I felt sorry for him, until he told me to clean out this old van which he'd bought off a traveller. I opened the back of it and among the rubbish was a great big dead rat with flies buzzing all over it.

♪ 9 ♪

Budding Pop Stars & Parties

We all meet up at the church hall on the Thursday night and nobody is late. So, let's introduce the band.

On drums is Tony who works in a music shop in Romford, which is handy as he can get all the gear we need at knockdown prices, especially the secondhand stuff. He's 17, tall and wiry with short, cropped, blonde hair, and is a good leader and organiser. The girls he goes out with are out of the ordinary, you know the type, very pale makeup, clothes that don't fit, hair that is in all shades of colours, in other words not the norm. Tony's given up playing with The Tellstars, which Johnny Brewster wasn't happy about – tough for him, but great for us. Steve plays bass but fancies lead guitar, he's got no chance. The only problem with him is he's good looking, with fair hair, a smart dresser and is in demand with the girls. Me? Well, I have my moments with the girls; I'm tall with dark hair and dress more Mod than the rest of the band. Rick is 18 and is one of those blokes that it doesn't matter what he wears, he always looks great. He has one of those smiles that melts the girls' hearts and their knickers. He works for Andrea's dad as a clerk in a stockbroker's office in the City of London.

ਡੇ ਡੇ ਡੇ

The first thing we needed was a name for the band. We came up with all sorts of names but couldn't agree until Tony said,

'We all like Mod music and we've all got a bit of an edge to us, so why don't we call ourselves 'Modern Edge'? And that's how we got our name.

We all realised that if we wanted to be an original band we'd have to play our own material and back it up with some covers. None of us were into real heavy rock, so that made life easier; if you can't agree on the type of music you want to play there's no use starting a band. We also had to be flexible by playing all types of music to keep everybody happy. Tony had written quite a lot of his own material but had done nothing with it. Me and Steve had put together a few numbers which needed a lot of work done on them. One of them was called 'Suburban Mod' which we felt was half decent.

It was fortunate we could all read music well. The only way we'd know whether we could make it was to go out and do a few dances. In any band there's a prime mover, who in some way organises from the front and we all agreed that Tony was the man.

Like any other band we wanted a Number One hit, appear on *Ready, Steady Go*, be a household name, earn lots of money, and meet as many girls as possible. We were really going for it and nothing was going to stop us.

Over the next few weeks we practised hard and put a couple of sets together, which included covers and original material. None of us let each other down, so much so we were ready to do a gig. In fact we had our first booking at La Nero coffee bar. We cemented our new relationship by going up the West End of London to see a band called Long John Baldry and the Hoochie Coochie Men. After the gig we treated ourselves to pie and mash with plenty of green liquor.

In between all the practising there were a number of parties to go to, with plenty of dancing, a few beers and lots of girls to chat up. There was a bit of trouble now and again, but it could be handled.

Another good friend, Alec, lived in a big old house with his mum and dad. He did like a party, and fortunately for us, his parents went away most weekends. The bonus was that his parents knew we had the parties there. Their thoughts were that they knew most of his friends, and as long as the place was tidy when they came home they didn't have a problem. It was important to us that we made sure that we left the house how we found it. At our parties there were between 20 and 40 people, any gatecrashers were soon sorted out and sent packing. Other times there were just half a dozen couples; these evenings were called 'The Half a Dozen Club', which was for very close friends only. There were six bedrooms in the house so everybody was happy. When you arrived Alec would tell you what bedroom you could use, if you were lucky. He called the bedrooms traps and he would say, 'You're in trap one, or trap two,' or whatever. This stopped anybody going into the wrong bedroom, when there was already a couple in there. Why did he call them traps? The family owned and trained greyhounds.

One of these club nights we'd booked our traps with Alec, me and Steve had met a couple of girls a few weeks before in a local coffee bar called The Bongo. Steve's girl was Val and mine was Joanne, who wore this perfume called Tigress, which was very alluring. Their dads were on the edge of criminality, and they were hard looking bastards, so it was a bit of a worry. They wouldn't take any prisoners if they felt their daughters were going out with a couple of randy Jack-the-lads who were trying to get them into bed. We put this out of our minds as we took the girls to Alec's place for the club night. They were suitably impressed by the grandeur of the house. The lounge was quite big and The Animals' number 'The House of the Rising Sun' was playing on the Dansette record player. Alec was a top lad and he welcomed us as usual; we supplied him with a couple of cans of Watney's Party Four beers. Alec had his girl, and Tony, Rod and Jimmy were there with their birds. We'd all have a little dance around, a few fags and a couple of beers and as the evening progressed, you hopefully could disappear with your girl into your trap and have a good time.

ﻬ ﻬ ﻬ

This particular evening everything's going to plan, for Steve anyway, as he drifts away with Val into trap two, and soon after I think I'm going to trap four. Unfortunately, Joanne tells me that the decorators are in (once a month) and there would be no nookie tonight. Never mind, we both make do on the large settee in the lounge, as we are the only couple left. I put on a Bobby Vinton record, 'My Heart Belongs to Only You'. Joanne is impressed with that, and she thinks I'm being very romantic. Well I was, wasn't I? As it happens I liked Joanne, she's a good laugh and we settle down for a quiet evening on the settee listening to music, having a Woodbine, a few beers, and hopefully an occasional moment of passion. Then, only a few minutes later, after everybody has disappeared upstairs, there's a yell from one of the bedrooms. Joanne and I rush upstairs, and I can hear Tony shouting out,

'Help. Help, I've caught me Hampton in the zip.'

Everybody rushes into his bedroom in a state of undress. Poor Tony is lying there on the bed with his dick caught in the zip of his Levi jeans, it's going redder and redder by the minute and it looks like a stick of rock. His girlfriend is hiding underneath the blanket, laughing her head off. Have you ever been in a situation when you don't know what to do for the best? I'm certainly not going to get my hands round his todger, that's for sure. All the other couples are laughing, as Tony is yelling the house down. Then one of the girls, Bev, a trainee nurse, walks forward and says to Alec,

'Get me a pair of gloves and some antiseptic.'

Within a minute Alec rushes back with a pair of pink Marigolds and some TCP. She puts the gloves on and starts to go to work on Tony's problem. Most of us can't watch as she expertly releases the zip from his todger. The relief on Tony's face is like he's won the football pools; everybody claps and then falls about laughing. Then Bev takes the TCP off Alec and dabs the broken skin with a paper hanky. He jumps up in the air when it hits the spot and screams the house down.

ᴥ ᴥ ᴥ

After that Tony only bought jeans and trousers with button flies. To be fair to him, a few days later he took Bev a bottle of Tweed perfume to say thank-you. When he found out that her mum and dad were out he asked whether she could check that his todger was healing up. She said with a laugh,

'No problem, it probably needs some more TCP dabbed on it anyway.'

Tony was away within seconds.

As I was saying, there were a lot of parties going on. In fact, a few weeks later, all the gang met at a pub on a Sunday lunchtime, before we went to Southend for the afternoon. The jukebox in the corner was thumping out 'A Hard Day's Night' by The Beatles. There were a couple of parties this coming Saturday and we were all working out which ones we were going to. Rod and Carol were going to one in Norwich with Jimmy and Diane. They'd met a couple at Margate on their last Bank Holiday trip whose party it was. Wendy and Roger were going to Liverpool to see some family. The rest of us, Ronnie, Steve, Tony and me were attending The Half a Dozen Club evening at Alec's house. We'd all lined up our current girlfriends and as luck would have it all the girls got extensions to stay out till midnight. If you got them home later than that, their parents were knocking on your door, or even worse, they were confined to barracks for a week or two. The only exception to the rule was when they could go away on those Bank Holiday weekends, where they would certainly let their hair down, which was great for us.

The whole gang had a great time at Southend, especially when we went to the Kursaal Amusement Park on the seafront and went on all the attractions. It's said that the Kursaal was the world's first theme park. After having a burger at a Wimpy Bar, we made our way home.

The following Saturday nothing went to plan for me and Steve. Alec's house for the party was knocked into touch when his parents decided to stay at home, so it was no Half a Dozen Club tonight. The other part of the crowd went up to the Norwich party. On the Saturday night we picked up our latest girlfriends. My girl was Fran; she had a Pixie hairstyle, a great body and was a Mod with all the gear. She did look nice, especially her lovely eyes, which were made even nicer with Miners make-up. When I commented, she told me she'd bought the make-up from a shop in Regent Street in London. I thought I was going to do a bit of long-term courting with her as I really fancied her.

Steve's girl was Sally; she was the best mate of Fran. She was a fair sort with a Flip hairstyle and wore a red pvc mac with black buttons and white stiletto shoes. There were lots of places to take them to, but not where we wanted to go, if you get my meaning. We took them to our usual little pub out in the country. We must have liked them as we bought them two port and lemons and two packets of salt and vinegar crisps.

After a couple of drinks we stopped off at the lay-by for a tray of eggs. There were no eggs. This wasn't a good omen, as the old farmer could creep up on us and put us off our stroke. The night was a washout; it started to rain and it was cold in the motor. The girls made it quite clear that this wasn't the way they wanted to spend their Saturday night out, and they probably wouldn't be seeing us again. The rain was coming down in sheets and the motor sprang a leak from two of the window seals, and it was dripping all over Fran's new skirt. Then Sally got cramp in her leg and started to moan big time.

Me and Steve lit up two Woodbines and called it a night, then we took the girls home. We went back to my place and put the television on and watched *Steptoe and Son* with Wilfrid Brambell and Harry H. Corbett, and finally *Match of the Day* with Kenneth Wolstenholme.

♪ 10 ♪

Tragedy

The next morning mum brought up the Sunday morning newspaper and a cup of tea. I normally went straight to the back page, but for some reason I looked at the front page. It was all about a bad car crash. As I read it, I was absolutely mortified by what I was reading. I kept saying to myself, 'No, no, it can't be.'

The phone rang; mum picked it up and shouted,
'It's Steve and it's urgent.'

I mumbled something about ringing him back in a minute. I started to read the report over and over again.

> On Saturday afternoon a minibus carrying seven people was involved in a crash near Norwich. Tragically a brother and sister were killed outright. Another passenger is in a serious condition, and four others have escaped with cuts and bruises.

I didn't read anymore, I knew it was Rod and Carol. I felt sick in the pit of my stomach. In the background the phone kept ringing and ringing and mum kept saying it was so and so, it just went over my head until Steve turned up. Steve told me that the seriously injured person was Jimmy and he was in a bad way. At times like this you go back to the last time you saw them – last Sunday we'd all been to Southend and had had a great day. When I said goodbye to Carol on that Sunday night she looked great. I remember I'd been poking fun at the long white winkle-pickers she was wearing. When I dropped her and Rod off, she kissed me on the cheek and said,

'Good night, sweet dreams, Nick.'

Rod was his usual self and said,

'Give you a ring when we're back from the party and we'll meet up for a drink.'

I remember they both waved to us as we left.

That was the last time we saw them alive. They were fun-loving people and died in their prime. One minute they were there laughing and enjoying life and the next minute, gone.

Diane came home from the hospital and, of course, we went to visit her. She remembered very little about the accident, which was probably a good thing. As if this wasn't tragic enough, Jimmy died in hospital a few weeks later from his injuries.

When they buried my best friends Rod and Carol, and their coffins were lowered into the ground at the local cemetery, I knew it was something I would never ever forget. Their poor mother and father, what could you say to them? I've never shed so many tears as that day. It was just as bad when we went to Jimmy's funeral. As you get older, you attend more funerals and shed more tears, till somebody sheds tears over you. When you leave this world, hopefully you'll have left some happy memories for the people you've left behind as Carol, Rod and Jimmy had.

♪ 11 ♪

Gigs, Girls & Bonfires

The first gig of Modern Edge at La Nero went down really well and was well supported by our friends. We all felt guilty about enjoying ourselves after the deaths of Rod, Carol and Jimmy. The guv'nor of the coffee bar, Ted, put all the profits for the evening and our gig money towards a charity that Carol had supported. Diane was very quiet and looked lost, which was to be expected after the trauma she'd suffered. Wendy and Roger kept close to her all evening as did the rest of the gang. Rick on vocals was ace, he could really sing. Andrea was there but we made sure she got nowhere near the microphone.

Watching was a guy who'd just opened a new dance hall called The Shelter at Upminster. It was like a long air-raid shelter, where live bands played. There was no alcohol, just soft drinks. The atmosphere was fantastic and it was one of those places you couldn't get enough of. You danced the night away or just listened to the band. After our gig he came over to us and offered us a residency there every other Friday night. The next Friday we went there to suss it out and to meet some girls. The band playing that night was called JC Four, who sounded fair. Rick was with Andrea and she was over him like a rash, but I could see he had other ideas for the future. He'd been going out with her for two years and hadn't sampled the fruits of life much, which was in abundance at The Shelter that night. When you're as good-looking as him, it's a shame not to share it. I could sense a fall for Andrea in the near future.

We met these two local girls who were a bit posh and lived in a smart area of Upminster. Steve's girl was Kim and mine was Delia, who wore these big clip-on plastic earrings, a nice short white skirt, and white sling-back shoes with kitten heels, which she said had cost her nearly five quid. I could've bought three pairs of shoes for that price and still have had change. She was also wearing a bottle green leather jacket which must have cost a fortune. We had a nice evening, with plenty of dancing and a few nibbles on the slow numbers. Of course we told them that our band was playing here next Friday and they were well impressed. We offered to take them home like you do, which they declined, because one of their dads was picking them both up.

'Can we see you tomorrow, then?' I said.

They had a little chat and surprise, surprise they said yes. We went out with them for a few weeks, and a couple of really funny things happened with them. Steve's girl, Kim, had these really strict parents who wouldn't let her go out until she'd done her college homework. She wasn't having this, so she'd climb out of her bedroom window onto a ledge above the front door, and then jump onto a privet bush below, so she could go and meet Steve. Steve was unaware of this, but he always wondered why she had scratches on her arse. Kim's dad was getting really annoyed with this dent on top of his bush, which was getting bigger everyday, and he couldn't fathom out what was causing it. His whole world was his garden and this was really winding him up. So one night he decided to hide in the garden with a big spade to find out what was causing it. Steve went to meet Kim and got there a bit early. He looked out of the car window and saw Kim opening her window. He was gobsmacked as she got out of her bedroom window onto the ledge over the front door and jumped into the privet bush. Unfortunately, on this occasion she got stuck in the bush. Steve got out of the motor and went over to help her. As he was pulling her out of the bush, her dad rushed over to them with this big shiny spade shouting abuse at them both. Somehow Steve pulled her clear from the bush and they both dashed to the motor and belted up the road with her old man chasing behind them. Kim was confined to barracks for a couple of weeks after that.

Sometime later we all went round to Delia's house. Her parents were going out that evening and they wanted to meet us to make sure we were respectable. Me and Steve both had a bath and wore our best mohair suits, button-down shirts, and put our pork pie hats on. About six o'clock that evening Steve, Kim and myself were taken by Delia into her kitchen, which was bigger than my house. In a corner there was a large cage with a macaw parrot called Freddie in it; it looked a mean old bird and was squawking out loudly. Delia had told us previously that it was her mum's and she thought the world of it. It didn't like her dad or any men, and when her mum wanted to be in the kitchen on her own she'd let it out of the cage to fly around. One day her dad forgot about this and went into the kitchen. The parrot, seeing his prey, dived at him; her dad had to go to hospital to have four stitches put into his ear. Delia told us that, after this, whenever her mother was out of the house her dad would go up to the cage and teach the parrot some swear words, which didn't go down too well with her mum.

Her parents came into the kitchen and we took our pork pie hats off as they entered, they seemed impressed with that. Freddie the parrot, on spotting Delia's dad, greeted him with 'Freddie is a wanker, Freddie is a wanker.' Her mum went ballistic and we wet ourselves with laughter. We had our tea in china cups and saucers. They weren't impressed when I poured some of the tea into the saucer to drink, as it was a bit hot. We'd just finished our tea and her parents were just about to go out. Me and Steve couldn't wait; it was going to be a great night. Suddenly Freddie let out this loud screech, we looked up and there he was on the perch, rigid.

Delia's mother screamed, 'Freddie, Freddie.'

It fell off its perch and landed on the bottom of the cage.

'It's dead, my Freddie's dead,' she cried.

Her dad had this big grin on his face when she said it. She looked at her husband and said,

'Do something Albert, please.'

So Albert, who was now really happy this dreaded bird was deceased, went over to the cage and took it out. To get some brownie points he opened its beak and attempted to blow air into its mouth. It wasn't working. He tried once more and then all hell let loose. Freddie came back to life and his beak was locked onto Albert's nose. He was yelling out in pain and tried to yank it off. There was blood everywhere and the murder of a parrot was about to take place, so the four of us disappeared quickly up the pub to escape the mayhem.

Our debut at The Shelter on the Friday was nearly a disaster. We'd just started playing a twelve-bar instrumental, and we were concentrating really hard on getting it right. Suddenly these flashing lights were switched on which caused a commotion on the dance floor. We stopped playing; no wonder the girls were upset. These bright lights were exposing all of the girls' underwear, especially anyone who was wearing white or very light colours. In some cases they had no underwear on, it was handsome. We saw one girl with a white lace dress and short sleeve blouse with the full works on show, suspenders, stockings the lot. The blokes couldn't take their eyes off the girls, as they ran off the floor in all directions. The girls wouldn't come back onto the dance floor until the lights were turned off. It took a few numbers before we got back into the groove but it went really well after that.

As expected, Rick packed up Andrea and went out with the girl with the white lace dress. The only downside for him was that Andrea's old man gave him the sack from his firm, as he wasn't going out with his daughter anymore, so he was looking for another job. Rick had certainly fallen on his feet with this new girl as she had her own Mini. This was unheard of in 1964, as girls very rarely had their own cars or even drove then. Within a few days Rick got a job as a salesman at a television rental company.

We did this gig at a church hall youth club in Chelmsford one Saturday night. We got the gig through our local vicar at the hall where we practised. He'd recommended us to this other vicar who was a mate of his. We loaded up the gear and we're off to the county town of Essex. Of course there's no alcohol at this club so we took some bottled beers with us. We thought it would be some rickety old place. What a surprise when we got there, it was a brand new building and massive. The vicar introduced himself to us and said that he'd sold all the tickets and there'd be a lot of people coming tonight. While we were talking to him, a couple of lovely looking girls, who looked like twins, gave us a wave. They immediately got four waves back from the band. We set up on the stage and were ready to play. What a night it was. As soon as we started with a Beatles' number, 'Love Me Do', everybody got up and danced. It was great playing to all these people, who were having a good time. We finished the first set with 'Sweets For My Sweet' by The Searchers. We sat on the stage and swigged our beer out of Tizer bottles, as we didn't want to upset the vicar that night, as we wanted our £5 gig money later. Now, as you do, we're looking out for some girls, and who should come over to us, but the twins who waved to us when we first came in. There were another two girls with them. The twins, who were really good-looking, were called Jane and Jenny. They now had Tony and Rick breathing all over them, so they'd pulled. The twins said we could all go back to their house for a party after the gig, as their parents wouldn't be home till later. The other two girls, Sandra, who I'd chatted up, and Pat, who was now with Steve, were up for a party, so things were looking up. We made arrangements to see them after the dance.

The second set went really well, but our minds were on the party. We finished the gig at ten o'clock sharp and the gear was in the van within 15 minutes, with the help of the four girls. The twins lived behind the church youth club. We went up to the house, and I pointed out to Steve a sign for 'The Vicarage'. Rick and Tony hadn't seen it, so why tell them the good news. Me and Steve started grinning at each other. When we entered the house we heard this gurgling noise coming from under the stairs. It seemed funny but we thought nothing more of it. Within minutes the Dansette record player was on and we were dancing to the Crystals' number, 'Then He Kissed Me'. The only downside, there was no alcohol, except for the twins' dad's homemade wine. So we had a few glasses of elderberry wine, which wasn't bad. The night was progressing well for Tony and Rick as they took the twins upstairs. As they went out of the room there was this feckin' great explosion; I thought a plane had dropped on top of the house. Rick, Tony and the twins ran back into the room looking stunned. They were covered head to foot in elderberry wine. Me and Steve and our two girls couldn't stop laughing. Then it got worse, the front door opened, and the vicar and his wife walked into the lounge. The look on Rick and Tony's face as the vicar entered the room was wicked. To say he was unhappy was an understatement, he went absolutely bonkers. He kicked us all out of the house, and we could hear him shouting at the twins as we legged it back to the van. The twins had thought that their parents would take at least two hours to tidy up the hall after the dance.

Rick contacted the twins later, and they said that there had been a couple of vats of elderberry wine fermenting under the stairs. The gurgling noise we heard was the wine on the move, and somehow it exploded. We never got invited back to the youth club to play again; I wonder why?

Tony booked up all our gigs because he was more organised than the rest of us. Initially, Rick said he wanted to do it, so we let him. These are the two reasons why Tony took over. Rick got this great booking, he told us, another fiver on top of what we normally charged, so we were well happy. He said he got a phone call from this bloke who'd seen us play and wanted to book us for his youth club. When Rick gave him our price for the gig, he said it wasn't enough, so he added an extra fiver on. Rick told us this gig was in Warley, near Brentwood in Essex, which was well handy, as it was just a few miles from where we all lived. So we loaded the van up with all our gear and went to this youth club. When we got there it was all locked up, and it stayed locked. About an hour later Rick's dad turned up and said to Rick,

'There's been a bloke on the phone ranting and raving and wanting to know why you're not there.'

To cut a long story short the gig was in Warley in Birmingham, not Essex. When we confronted Rick he said he wondered why the bloke had a Brummie accent. When he offered directions to his youth club, Rick said he knew where it was, thinking it was just around the corner from where he lived. The bloke had seen us play at a pub when he'd visited his son in Romford and that's why he was giving us the extra money, for the petrol!

The next gig he booked was a pub, which had a real bad reputation. We turned up early at this place and started setting up. We'd just finished when a bunch of Rockers turned up and start yelling and shouting at us. Then they started slinging punches and kicking our gear about. We weren't having that so of course we gave them plenty back, and as they were getting the worst of it, they left the pub with a few cuts and bruises. Good old Rick had put the wrong date in the diary, we were supposed to be there the following week and of course the Rockers were the band that was supposed to be playing that night.

Out of the blue a company got in touch with us to see whether we could do a gig for them in a few days' time. Another band had let them down badly, and they were in trouble. The money they offered us was a lot more than we normally charged and as we didn't have a gig on that date, we of course said yes. It was a private party for about 80 people from a company in London. It was being held on an old Thames sailing barge which was sailing from a port in Essex. The barge was going out on the morning tide, and coming back later that night. We turned up and unloaded the gear, which was a big problem, as it had to be taken downstairs into the hold. I wasn't too happy about this booking as I used to get seasick on paddle boats in the park when I was a kid. We finally got the gear down and what a sight greeted us. The hold was massive and it was all festooned with decorations and looked great. One of the organisers made himself known to us and we set up our gear. There were a number of waitresses who were serving the guests on the trip; they wore captain's hats and black and white uniforms, which were quite skimpy. As luck had it Rick knew one of the girls and straight away we were given plenty of drinks. Most of the people on board were Hooray Henrys who were very loud and boisterous. We started playing and it was soon apparent that the music wasn't a priority for the revellers; it was how much booze they could get down their throats. Within an hour they'd drunk the boat dry and when it ran out, they went mad and started causing damage to the boat. It got so bad that the captain radioed the police for help. They sent out a launch to escort the barge back to port, where the police were waiting for them. They talk about the trouble with Mods and Rockers, but this lot were something else. For us, it was great news; we'd got paid up front for only two hours work and later that night, we took four of the waitresses out, and had our own party.

For the rest of the year we had plenty of bookings and we were also playing further afield in Kent, Suffolk and Hertfordshire. This was causing havoc with our football commitments, and all aspects of our social and work life. A lot of the bookings were coming from Tony's boss, Mick, who owned the music shop. Mick also ran an agency for bands and this was taking up more of his time than the shop. A decision had to be made for us, as to which way the group was heading. The decision was made easier for all of us as Mick was thinking of selling the shop, which would put Tony out of a job.

We used an old Ford van to travel around in. It was a heap, but it did the job. We knew it might have to go soon, because every time we went through a puddle we got wet feet, so we were on the look-out for another one.

A couple of days before bonfire night I was at work and you could see Eddie had other things on his mind. All the decent motors had disappeared over night from the car lot, which had included a nice little red Heinkel Bubble car; all that was left was a pile of rubbish, except for a big old Commer van which was in good nick. It looked like he'd added some other motors, which, in my eyes he must have got straight from the scrapyard. When I asked the question about where they'd all gone, Eddie just fobbed me off. Later that day he took me to one side and had a chat.

'How's your band going?'

'It's going well,' I replied.

Eddie pointed to the Commer van. 'How would you like that for the band?'

'You're joking,' I said, 'We can't afford that.'

'You leave that to me. Now, where are you on bonfire night?'

'I'll be up my local, *The Queens Arms* in Parkfield, from about nine o'clock onwards.'

I thought that was a funny question to ask, but it was easy to answer. November 5th to me and Steve was a very important event of the year. When we were younger, bonfire night was a community event. We kids would start putting the bonfire together in August when we were on school holidays. Where we lived, there was a field at the back of the houses where we'd build the bonfire. The whole street would get involved. We'd collect the wood from wherever we could get it from. We were a bit naughty; on the other side of the field was a lot of posh houses with stuck-up kids, and to them we were the roughs. Me and Steve and a few other local kids would creep over to their bonfire and nick all their wood or we'd set it alight the day before bonfire night. We'd dress up one of our friends, Lennie, as a guy, as he was the smallest. We'd put him on a homemade cart, wheel him up the local shops, and ask for a penny for the guy, this helped pay for our fireworks and fags. Nobody knew he wasn't a dummy, until he lit up a Player's Anchor tipped and set himself alight. The straw on his hat and clothes caught fire and one of the local shopkeepers had to throw a bucket of water over him to put it out. He was a game lad, Lennie, and it didn't put him off as he dressed up again with fresh straw the next day. We had to go down a steep hill to get to the shops, and unfortunately the boy who was pushing him let go. The cart gathered speed down the hill and Lennie was holding on for dear life when one of the wheels came off. The cart hurtled across the road and smashed into a fence, making a right old mess. Lennie was thrown from the cart, and the bloke who owned the fence came storming out of his house; he saw his broken fence and the cart smashed to bits. Looking further he saw what he thought was a dummy guy. In a fit of rage he was just about to kick the bollocks out of the guy, when Lennie screamed out,

'No, no, I'm real, not a dummy.'

'If that's the case you can feckin' pay for the fence.'

We always attended the bonfire celebrations down our street; even at 17 we still had that community spirit. People would live in the same street for years, and we knew everybody. We'd roast potatoes and chestnuts in the fire embers and a bottle of pop and sparklers were given to the kids.

I didn't think any more of it until Eddie turned up at the pub on bonfire night.

'What are you doing here?' I asked.

'Just passing, Nick,' he replied.

He bought me and Steve a drink and was quite chatty. I noticed he kept looking at his watch. About 9.30 the pub phone rang and the landlord, Larry, answered it. He shouted out,

'Is there an Eddie Tucker here?'

Eddie made himself known and went behind the jump to answer it. Within a couple of minutes he was back.

'What's all that about, Eddie, and how'd they know you're here?' I asked.

'I've got a bit of bad news.'

'What's the matter, mate?'

'The car lot, portakabin and all of the motors have been set alight, burnt to the ground, they reckon it could've been a stray rocket.'

I looked at Steve, then Eddie and we all burst out laughing. Hang about! That meant I hadn't got a job. Eddie seemed chipper as he bought three pints of Double Diamond and three Cutty Sark whisky chasers.

'What's all this mean then, Eddie?' I asked.

'Well, I haven't got a business now,' he then bursts out laughing. 'But I'm well insured, in fact I've got so much insurance money I should be able to retire for a bit.'

'What about me? I can't retire. I've got my road tax and insurance to pay next week, plus all the overheads that a 17-year-old has.'

Steve, in his usual supportive manner, said, 'How's Nick going to buy his Johnnies, Double Diamond, and Woodbines?'

'Yeah, I was coming to that,' replied Eddie.

'I'm glad you are.' I said.

'Unfortunately, you're out of a job,' he said as he looked at his watch. 'Twenty minutes ago, Nick.'

'I'm well chuffed with that, Eddie. Your loyal employee for over two years through thick and thin. Do you remember that afternoon you were humping that petrol pump attendant in the portakabin when your missus turned up? I stopped her going in, I said we had an infestation of mice and were waiting for the pest control bloke to come, and what about ...'

'Okay, Nick, point taken. You'll be looked after. Here's the key for that Commer van that was in the yard, you can have it for your band. It's outside and it's yours for nothing.'

He then handed me a brown envelope.

'There's a good few quid in there for you as well. That'll see you through for a few weeks. My accountant will send you your cards, and before you ask, the Commer is not a cut and shut, I got it off a vicar who runs a youth club.'

Suddenly a bloke walked into the pub and stood by the doorway. You could smell the smoke on him, and if you couldn't, the singed eyebrows and burnt hair gave the game away. Eddie finished his pint in one gulp, shook hands with me, said 'Be lucky,' and he disappeared out of the door with him, never to be seen again.

So I was out of work and Tony wasn't sure how long his job was going to last, so decisions were going to have to be made. The band decided to have a chat with Mick to see whether he could put a few more gigs our way so we could go full-time. Even though they had jobs both Rick and Steve were up for it. Mick was in his thirties, a cool dude as they say, and drove a Lotus Elan, so he must have had a few bob. Tony said he was someone to be trusted and he'd worked for him for two years. The upshot of it all was that he was selling his music shop, and was now concentrating on promoting and managing bands. He felt we could go far and he wanted to manage us.

This is where Rick came in handy – when we got a contract, we showed it to Rick's dad. His father ran a very large haulage business in Essex and was smart. He went over it with a fine toothcomb, and after showing it to his solicitor and accountant said it was sound. My dad said,

'Go for it, Nick. You're only 17 and if it doesn't work out, it won't be the end of the world, but don't forget to pay your mother £1 a week for your upkeep.'

We were under contract for just one year, and after that both parties could go their separate ways. We were both new to the business, us as a band and Mick as an agent, promoter and manager.

We had a final meeting and all agreed to go for it. So at the end of 1964 the decision was made that we'd go full-time with the band. We all wondered what 1965 would bring. The final gig of the year was on New Year's Eve. We played at a dance hall in East London, and it was nearly our last. There were a lot of Rockers there and they were not impressed as we were a Mod band. We tried to play a bit more Rock 'n' Roll to keep them happy and it looked like we'd succeeded until Tony let go of one of his drum sticks on the last number, which was Johnny Kidd and The Pirates' 'Shakin' All Over'. The stick hit a nearby Rocker right in the face, then it all kicked off, it was the excuse they'd wanted. The Rocker and about eight others rushed on to the stage and started knocking the shit out of us. We tried to fight back the best we could, but we took a bit of a pasting and so did our equipment, for the second time! The bouncers saved us from getting seriously hurt, but we all had to go to hospital with cuts and bruises. Rick had to stay in overnight as he had concussion. Some of the kit was ruined and we weren't insured. After that we got all our gear insured. It was touch and go whether we could afford to go on, but one punch up wasn't going to put us off our goal to be a top chart band.

1965

Goldie, a golden eagle, escapes from London Zoo and enjoys 13 days of freedom.

Winston Churchill dies at the age of 90.

The Post Office tower opens in London.

'Mrs Brown, You've Got A Lovely Daughter' by Herman's Hermits reaches No.1 in the charts.

Malcolm X is assassinated in New York City.

The film of Dr Zhivago is premiered.

Freddie Mills, former British boxing champion, is found shot in his car in Soho.

Soviet Alexei Leonov performs the first space walk.

Singer Nat 'King' Cole dies.

One millionth Mini is produced.

India invades West Pakistan.

English model Jean Shrimpton introduces the miniskirt to Australia at Derby Day in Melbourne.

Ronnie Scott opens his jazz club in Frith Street in London.

Stan Laurel of comedy duo Laurel & Hardy dies, aged 74.

American aircraft bomb North Vietnam.

The Beatles collect their MBEs from Buckingham Palace.

Mont Blanc tunnel linking France and Italy opens.

Ian Brady & Myra Hindley are charged with the Moors Murders.

ITV bans cigarette commercials.

Great Train robber Ronald Biggs escapes from prison.

The 70mph speed limit is introduced.

Broadcaster Richard Dimbleby passes away.

The first episode of Thunderbirds is shown.

Stanley Matthews retires from first-class football.

♫ 12 ♫

Band on the Move

The beginning of 1965 and we were a full-time band. We had to make sure we all had the right musical equipment. With Mick having sold his music shop, he let us have some instruments at knock-down prices. Mind you, with all the equipment that was ruined in the punch up in East London, we had to borrow a lot of money to help pay for the new guitars, drum kit, amplifiers and speakers. We were lucky; I got myself a Fender Musicmaster guitar, Steve got a Hofner bass guitar and Tony had a nice Ludwig drum set. We got a mixture of Vox AC30 and Selmer amplifiers, and Rick had a top-of-the-range Shure microphone. Rick, unknown to us, could play keyboards, which was a real bonus. My guitar cost an absolute fortune, but my grandma had remembered me in her will, so I thought that was money well spent, and it would always remind me of her. The places we were playing at were all within a reasonable reach of our home base, so we could get back at night with no added expense for B&B. The van had the name of the group plastered all over it, and we were on the move to make the charts or so we thought.

In between the music, Steve had fallen back in love with Vicky, the one who I'd said had pyorrhoea.

❧ ❧ ❧

One day I get this phone call from Steve, who is at Vicky's house, and he doesn't sound very happy. He asks me if I'll go round straight away. As he's my best mate, I jump straight into the motor and head for her house. I knock on the door and I'm thinking to myself, what's going on here. I'm greeted by a crying Vicky and a worried Steve. Fortunately, her parents are out. Then the unhappy story unfolds and I'm doing my Marjorie Proops bit. We both light up and draw hard on one of those horrible Domino cigarettes that you bought in a packet of five when you were skint and really desperate.

'We think she's up the duff,' says Steve.

Vicky starts howling and sobbing uncontrollably. I had been watching *Dr. Kildare* on the television before coming out; I didn't know which was worse.

'Vicky, when was the last time the decorators were in?' I ask.

'I don't know what you mean,' she said, 'We've had no decorators in. My dad does it all himself.'

'What he means, Vicky, is when was your last monthly?'

'I don't know Steve, about seven weeks ago, I suppose.' She starts howling again.

'I'm going to be a dad,' shouts Steve.

'I'm going to be a mum,' wails poor Vicky.

In a moment of stupidity I say, 'Can I be the godfather?' This doesn't go down too well.

'I don't want a baby, Steve, we've got to do something about it, what can we do?' she says.

'Yeah, what can we do?' replies Steve.

We all look at each other, it's the blind leading the blind.

'How'd you know you're pregnant, Vicky?' I ask.

'I just do.'

'Take me home Nick,' says Steve, 'I can't cope with all this.'

'What about me, Steve? You're a great help. How'd you think I feel? My mum and dad will kill me and probably you as well.'

'It is mine, Vicky?' asks Steve.

Vicky loses it, and tells Steve his life history in one line. It's all getting a bit fraught, but I manage to calm it down and we make arrangements to see Vicky the following day and come up with a solution.

The next day me and Steve are having a cup of Camp coffee round my house and mum brings out two large portions of home-made bread pudding. Steve's off his grub so I have both pieces. He isn't impressed when I say he's now eating for two and should eat his bread pudding up. It's 1965 and who do you ask about such matters? Parents are out of the question, you wouldn't discuss sex with them. So where do you go? Sid the barber, he seems to know about these things. He loves it when me and Steve turn up for his advice; he is salivating as he tries to prise out all the sexual details from Steve.

'How'd you get her up the spout then, Steve?' asks Sid.

'Probably, because one of your poxy Johnnies split open.'

'Yeah, I did have a bad batch, sorry about that.'

When he says that, Steve nearly gets hold of his turkey neck to bounce him all over his barber's shop. Sid's answer is easy.

'A bottle of gin and a hot bath. If that doesn't work, another bottle of gin and throw her down the stairs, that'll do the trick, end of problem.'

Steve looks at me, we shake our heads in disgust and walk out of the shop.

We meet up with Vicky and suggest she goes to see her doctor for some advice. She's having none of it, so we give her two bottles of gin and tell her to have a hot bath. If that doesn't work, instead of throwing her down the stairs, we tell her to drink the gin and keep walking up and down the stairs until she's exhausted. That should do it.

❧ ❧ ❧

The next day Vicky's mum and dad went shopping. On their return they found their daughter lying soaking wet at the bottom of the stairs, with two empty bottles of gin, acute alcohol poisoning, and a swollen ankle. After a long hot bath, she'd walked up and down the stairs for two hours, and then fallen down them, pissed as a newt.

Vicky had a hangover which lasted well over a week and was on crutches for another two. Steve did eventually get to speak to her, and she told him that she'd found out that she hadn't been pregnant in the first place, it was a false alarm.

Vicky decided Steve wasn't for her, and you couldn't blame her. And as his best mate, I wasn't much good either.

♫ 13 ♫

Ronnie, Irons, The Gas Board & Pigs

We supplemented our wages from the band with anything we could earn a few bob from. But nothing could prepare me for a phone call that came out of the blue from Ronnie (The Iron) Dicks. How he got the nickname The Iron is funny. A couple of years back, he was having his once-a-week bath, and shouted out to his mum,

'Could you iron my shirt for me?'

His mum was already ironing the shirt at the top of the stairs, next to the bathroom, when there was a knock on the front door; Mrs Dicks went downstairs to answer it. Ronnie didn't get an answer from his mum so he shouted out again,

'What about that ironing?'

His very young brother heard the word 'iron', so he lifted the Morphy Richards iron off the board and took it into Ronnie thinking he wanted it. Ronnie was bending over the bath taking the plug out. What happened, the young boy made contact with Ronnie's arse and the iron branded him for life.

Ronnie and his family were a bunch of rogues. He lived with his parents, four brothers and two sisters, and money was always tight. His other nickname was Ronnie the Meter. They were one of the lucky ones, they had a brand new council house with gas fires. We were still on coal fires in our house. Of course you've got to pay for the gas, but in their house they didn't. It was the time when if you knew what you were doing you could turn the meter around, so instead of the meter going forwards and giving you a bill, it went backwards. The problem with that was that if you forgot to turn it back to normal you went beyond your last reading and no gas was used. They were the only family I knew that had their gas cooker and fires on full in the summer months with every door and window wide open to get rid of the heat to burn some gas. You couldn't let the gasman into the house, otherwise he would suss it out. It got so bad he tried to reverse the meter back to start charging for gas again. Unfortunately, Ronnie messed about with it too much and created a gas leak. Thank goodness he got everybody out of the house before the explosion!

Back to the phone call from Ronnie, we didn't have a gig that night, so I was watching *The Likely Lads* on a small Bush black-and-white telly; it was like watching TV on a postage stamp. I was settled down for the night with a bag of Smith's potato crisps with the little blue bag of salt and a few Mackeson beers. Mum thought I looked a bit peaky and said I need some Virol, whose motto was: 'For those who are flagging'. I thought a Mackeson stout sounded better. Ronnie was a wheeler and dealer, and was into anything to make a few quid. He was a staunch guy, but there was always an edge to him which you had to look out for.

'Would you like to earn a few bob tonight?' he asked.

'Well, I'm always interested in a couple of bob, Ronnie.'

'I'll be round in half an hour.'

Before I could ask him what it was, the phone went dead.

ॐ ॐ ॐ

He turns up in this little old Ford Anglia which was in a right old state. I got in and Ronnie has Radio Luxembourg on, and bloody Horace Batchelor is going on about his football pools schemes. His final words were always: 'Department One, Keynsham, spelt K-E-Y-N-S-H-A-M, near Bristol.' We've both had enough of that, so put on another radio station and listen to 'Cast your Fate to the Wind' by Sounds Orchestral. I'm thinking to myself that's not a good omen for tonight. Ronnie says,

'All we've got to do is pick up a consignment of meat for a butcher friend of mine and there's two quid in it for you. It should only take an hour.'

Two quid for an hour's work is worth having, so I'm well up for it. I'm thinking it must be a cold storage place, as we're going onto an industrial estate at the back end of Rainham. At the end of this estate there's a dirt track which Ronnie reverses down about 100 yards. There's a large farm gate and behind that there are some outhouses. As he turns the car lights off, Ronnie says,

'Keep quiet and I'll whistle when I need you, and be on your toes.'

He disappears with a torch in one hand and a big blanket in the other into the darkness. The penny should've dropped there and then but all I can see is two quid, I don't pick up on the danger signs. About five minutes later I hear this very loud squealing noise and then nothing. Then I hear a whistle and see a beam of light which is beckoning me towards it. On reaching Ronnie, he's grinning all over his face like some soft kid. At his feet is a blanket and something big is under it.

'Right, you ready to do a bit of lifting, then?'

'Hang about, Ronnie, what am I lifting?'

I pull the blanket back and there's this feckin' dead pig with its eyes wide open looking at me.

'What's bleedin' going on down here, Ronnie?'

'Keep your voice down, the geezer who owns this pig farm lives just around the corner. Now, lift up and let's get on our toes.'

So like some mug I lift up this lump of pork with Ronnie and start going back towards the motor. Halfway we both get a fit of giggles and have to stop. We've lost it now and we can't move for laughter. But the sound of dogs barking makes us move quickly back to the motor. Ronnie lifts the boot up and tries to put this porky in. It won't go. Ronnie starts to panic, as the dogs seem to be getting nearer. He undoes both doors to put it on the back seat.

'You're not going to put it in there surely, Ronnie?'

'Of course I am, I'm not leaving it here, I've spilt blood for this.'

We somehow lay it on the back seat, which makes the car go right down to the springs. Ronnie lays the blanket over the pig and we're off to the sound of 'Go Now' by The Moody Blues on the radio. We just keep laughing and looking at the back seat and making snorting noises. We're in the High Street on our way to a local butcher. Ronnie sees two girls by a bus stop, he pulls the motor up next to them.

'Where're you going, girls?' asks Ronnie.

'Hornchurch,' one of them says.

I can't believe it; trying to pull two birds and we've got a pig lying on the back seat, stone dead. These girls look a bit, how can I put it, well you wouldn't take them home to mum for afternoon tea. When Ronnie suggests that we can drop them off at Hornchurch they get straight in the back of the motor. As mentioned, the back seat is depressed right down by the weight of the pig, so when the girls jump in, they sit on the blanket which is covering Mr. Porky. Fortunately, the girls are small, but they do look a bit uncomfortable and slightly hunched up, but they don't seem to care much, as they're saving their shilling bus fare between them. Everybody is happy, except for the pig, as 'Baby Please Don't Go' by the band Them comes on the radio. It's going so well that we're going to take them for a drink, and some pork scratchings, until Ronnie puts his anchors on. He's come up to a Zebra crossing and some old boy jumps out in front of him. Ronnie stops just in time. Then the screaming starts. The sharp braking has dislodged the blanket covering the pig.

'What the bloody hell's that?' says one of the girls.

'It's a feckin' great pig', says her mate, 'I'm sitting on a dead pig.'

Ronnie and I look round and there's Mr. Porky's head on show with its tongue hanging out, eyes open and blood dripping onto the floor. The girls are hysterical and shouting, 'Let me out, let me out.'

They finally get out of the motor and start kicking it. We're creased up which makes the girls even wilder. It doesn't help when we stick our heads out of the window and start snorting. They give it one last kick and run off up the road. I've never laughed so much in my life. We finally move off to the butchers and I get paid my couple of quid, and the promise of some pork chipolatas.

ॐ ॐ ॐ

A couple of weeks later I was reading the local newspaper and there on the front page was the headline, 'Pig Rustling in Rainham.' One of Ronnie's mates had the same idea, and had been caught nicking pigs from the same place we went to. It was the first case of pig rustling in Rainham for over 50 years.

We were playing all kinds of gigs from pubs to dance halls, even weddings if they were paying. We had a booking once every two weeks at a pub in East London, it was a muck and bullets type of place, but they seemed to like us and it paid well. One Friday night, we were asked to do a number by this gorilla who had tattoos all over his face and weighed about 20 stone. He was one of those blokes that if he asked you to do something, you did it. The song was 'My Boy Lollipop' by Millie. It had been played a lot over the airwaves so we'd a rough idea of how to play it. Rick refused to sing it because it was so naff, so I got lumbered with singing. We started to play, then his girlfriend got out of her chair and began to dance to it on her own. Dancing to 'My Boy Lollipop' is as sad as it gets, but dancing on your own is even sadder. The girl was well built and had a massive pair of knockers; they bounced up and down like Barnes Wallis's bouncing bombs in *The Dambusters*. When she got on the dance floor everybody else got off. Her bloke loved seeing his girlfriend giving it the business but the problem was the dance floor was quite small and she was in your face. All the band's eyes were watching her, she did have a pair and she knew it. Anyway this went on every time we played there, and we were getting well fed up with 'My Boy Lollipop', we were losing our street cred. So the next time he asked us to play it, we did, but we played it four times during the evening. Of course she got up and danced four times. The punters were getting fed up of looking at her and hacked off with 'My Boy Lollipop' as much as we were. On the fourth time, the crowd really gave her some stick and she ran off crying. Her boyfriend couldn't fight the whole pub, so that was the last time we played that, ever.

Another time we did a gig as a favour to one of our mates and got done hook, line and sinker. He belonged to a fishing

club and it was their annual dinner and dance. When it came
to the money side of things, he said he would look after us.
After the dance he gives us four large fish each and said,

'This is better than money, you'll enjoy these.'

We weren't happy, but what could you do. I gave my mum
the fish for our tea on Friday night, which was always fish and
chips. I got home a bit late on the Friday after practising with
the band. I went straight to the table for my tea, mum brings
it in, and it's egg and chips.

'Where's my nice bit of fish, I was looking forward to
that.'

'Nick,' she said, 'I've never heard of anybody eating pike
and chips before?'

We were still trying to get some of our own material
together. Mick got us some studio time and we cut a few
demo tapes which weren't very good, so we binned them. He
also got us quite a bit of work and we were just about holding
our own on the money front, when we got some really good
news. One of his mainline groups which had made the
bottom end of the charts had disbanded when two members
left. This was a real bonus for us as they had a four-week tour
of the south-west of England already booked. Mick said we
could do it, and the money was top dollar. The four of us
jumped at the opportunity to go on tour, especially as it was
in the summer and there would be plenty of girls about. The
venues were much better than we were used to, so we felt we
were moving in the right direction. We had three weeks to get
our own material up to speed; you never knew who could be
listening.

14

On Tour with Big Al & Sampson

I met up with Big Al, the Rocker who we had met on our way to Brighton; we had a drink in the pub he frequented. I was in there a bit early and the jukebox was playing 'Three Steps to Heaven' by Eddie Cochran. The drinkers were all Rockers; I looked well out of place, and they were giving me the hard look. Fortunately, Al came in and the natives went back to drinking and playing snooker. I got the impression that he was the main face of the pack and what he said went. We had a good chat about playing football together in the district team and I reminded him about a game we played against Barking when they had a few players on West Ham's books. At 11 he had long hair down to his shoulders, and was shaving everyday with his dad's Remington. He was a big lump and everybody was scared of him, but we got on well. He was the centre half, I was left back, and our motto on the football field was: 'They will not pass.'

Barking had this tricky winger, called Billy, whose nickname was Billy Whizz; he was as quick as a fox and just as cunning, and you were always chasing him, you could never get close enough to put a tackle in. The game was the quarter final of the Pelly Cup, which was a premier cup competition in Essex and London. All the top players who'd graduated into the pro game would've played for their district team in this cup. We were playing at Hornchurch Stadium and there were a few hundred people watching. Billy Whizz was their main man and within a few minutes he'd nutmegged Big Al and placed the ball in our net. Billy Whizz then started to do some showboating whenever he got the ball. We had a quick chat when the ball went out of play. It was agreed that between us he'd have to go. A few minutes later he got the ball near the touch line and we made a beeline for him. He tried to do one of his party tricks to get past Big Al; in doing so Al went through him on a 50-50 ball, he went up in the air and as he came down I took him out with another tackle and he went flying over the wall into the stand. That was the end of Billy Whizz. He went off and didn't come back on the pitch. We won the game 3-1, but he had the last laugh; he went on to play professional football in Division One of the Football League.

We had a good laugh about it; it was great to see Big Al again. I talked about our band and told him we were touring the west country in a couple of weeks' time.

'Do you want somebody to drive the van for you?'

'What do you mean?' I said.

'Well, you want a bit of security with all the musical equipment you're carrying and I can be your roadie and help you set up. My brother plays in a band and I've helped him a few times.'

This sounded great as we were also thinking of taking a motor with us. We all wanted to sample the local talent and a Commer van isn't ideal to take them out for a spin.

'That'd be great', I said, 'But I doubt if we've enough money in the pot to pay you.'

'Don't worry, I know a few Rockers in the south-west, they'll see me all right.'

'I'll have to square it with our manager and the rest of the lads,' I replied.

Nobody had a problem with him coming, and in fact they

were really pleased as equipment was sometimes stolen on these tours. Having a big lump of a Rocker who could scare for Britain on your side was just what you wanted. I never asked what he did for a living. I did sort of semi ask, but he just said,

'A bit of this and a bit of that.'

This means he was probably at it, and best not to say anymore.

We were now off on our first tour – to celebrate, I bought a brand new pork pie hat, which was all the rage. Mum and Dad were there to wave us off. Between us we'd bought this tasty Ford Consul Mark II which was big enough to carry the band around. We were all waiting for Big Al to turn up; just then in the distance we could hear the rumble of motorbikes. We all looked up the road and so did the whole street, as everybody came out of their houses to have a look. The noise got nearer and there were shining lights. We all looked at each other and Steve said,

'Is it a UFO landing?'

As we looked again a big old Humber Super Snipe with Big Al in the passenger side was driving in front of about 30 motorbikes. They all stopped outside our house.

'I haven't got enough cups for all of them,' Mum said.

We all burst out laughing as he got out of the motor.

'The boys are giving me a send off,' he said.

We all relaxed as he took his gear out of the Humber and put it in the van. He then opened the back door of the motor and this feckin' great animal jumped out, I thought it must have escaped from a zoo, it was massive; I don't know whether the Doberman had shagged the Alsatian first or vice versa. It made Dash the Old English sheepdog in the Dulux paint advert look like a midget. Big Al said,

'Meet Sampson. I should've told you about him. When we're all tucked up in bed with our groupies, he's our security. Nobody is going to break into the van and nick your gear with him sleeping in there, are they?'

'Only if they're on a death wish,' said Rick.

'What do you feed it on?' asked Tony.

'You, if you don't take it for a walk once a day.'

'You're taking the mick.'

'Look, once he gets to know you, he's as good as gold.'

Tony moved on quickly and said, 'Right, let's get the show on the road to Bournemouth.'

15

Bournemouth & The ...

We made our way to the first gig at Bournemouth. As we were playing the following night we could take it easy on the journey. Mick told us that the gigs we were playing had nearly all sold out, so everyone was happy. He would be joining us later on the tour. We stopped halfway for breakfast at a transport café, lots of holidaymakers having the same idea. With 'Modern Edge' written all over the van, it created a bit of a stir, especially with the girls that were going on holiday with their parents. A few of them came over for a chat. Big Al took Sampson for a walk around the car park before we went in for our nosh. It had only gone a matter of yards when it cocked its leg up. Well, its dick was as big as a baby's arm and the flow was like a fountain. It then had a massive dump which came out steaming. It certainly put our new fan club off, as some of the girls started retching. It reminded me of when I went dog racing with Steve. Just before the race the dogs were paraded around the ring by the kennel maids. The dog in trap three, China Boy, had this enormous dump, so I thought it would feel better after that and put a few bob on it. The poxy thing came in last; probably all its energy had gone in that pile.

We arrived in Bournemouth, parked the Consul, while Big Al went to find the B&B that Mick had arranged. The rest of us had a walk along the seafront. We stopped to look at a notice board on the wall next to the tourist centre. We were well chuffed as there was a poster of us advertising the next night's gig. Further up the promenade was a big theatre. A very well-known chart band called The ... were playing that night, they were the new band on the block. By this time we were feeling a bit peckish and looking for a café. We walked up to the theatre and Rick said,

'I've got an idea, follow me and I'll do the talking.'

We didn't know what he was up to; he just walked off so we followed. At the entrance of the theatre we were stopped from going in by security, an old boy with thick-rimmed glasses.

'It's closed until tonight, lads.'

'Yeah, we know,' said Rick. 'We're The ... , we're playing here tonight; we've just arrived and want to see the stage before setting up.'

The rest of us were bemused and didn't know where this was taking us.

'How do I know you're The ... ?' he asked.

'There's a photo of us up on that poster,' Rick replied.

High up on a hoarding was a photograph of the group. We had our target tee-shirts on, and we did have a slight resemblance to the group who were wearing the same type of thing. The old boy looked up at this hoarding and then at us.

'Sorry, lads, didn't recognise you at first, come in, my granddaughter loves you lot.'

'That's cool,' said Rick. 'Did our management organise some food and drink for us?'

'It's all laid out in your dressing room. If you'd like to follow me, I'll take you there.'

Rick was a dark horse and he'd gone up in my estimation. I did remember the crab joke that he'd caught me out with, so he did have an edge to him. Now we could see where Rick was coming from and we played the pop star image to the full. The old bloke took us into a dressing room which was well tasty. There was a nice spread laid out on the table, and a few bottles of the local brew to wash it down with. We asked Rick how he knew that there would be food laid on.

'I didn't,' he said, 'just winged it.'

We polished the grub off in record time, and we were glad the old boy was short-sighted, otherwise we would've been sussed. He came back a few minutes later and noticed the food and drink had gone.

'Would you like some more?'

'That would be great mate', replied Rick, 'Could you ask the chef if they could put some Branston Pickle in the ham sarnies, I'm allergic to mustard.'

'Is your granddaughter coming tonight?' asked Tony.

'No, she can't afford the prices here and I haven't got that sort of money. As it is I've taken a night job to make ends meet.'

'Don't worry about that, mate,' said Tony. 'Here are two free tickets for her and her friend.'

The old boy was as happy as a peeping tom with three eyes, as he took the tickets off Tony.

'You've made my day, I can't wait to ring her and tell her the good news, the food will be here pronto,' and with that he went out of the door.

'Where'd you get those tickets from, Tony?' I asked.

'They were in the envelope on the other table; I suppose the band gets a few freebies.'

'How many in there?'

'Another six.'

'Well, that's our free entertainment for tonight, lads.'

The extra food was brought in by a youngish woman who looked us up and down.

'You've changed a lot from your photo outside,' she said.

'No, I'm still good looking,' said charmer Rick, 'The photograph was taken a while back.'

My best mate, Terry Page, and myself enjoying a day at the beach in the sixties. (Alan Hammond collection)

It's a Mods world on the beach at Brighton in May 1964. Were you there? (Step Back in Time)

Mods 'n' Rockers exchanging deckchairs at Brighton seafront in May 1964 (Step Back in Time)

(left above) Rockers Chris Edwards with Graham (Smoky) Hickman astride his Honda Dream motorbike in 1965. (Graham Hickman collection)

(left below) Sixties teenagers in Kent with their scooters. From left to right, John Dyer, Wendy Simmonds, Angela and Bob Cannon, and Pete Vickery. (Kent Photos, Roger Curd collection)

(above) Sixties girl Christine Hughes, with her bouffant hairstyle, stands in front of a Mini. No wonder I married her. (Alan Hammond collection)

(left) Two Mod girls – Judy Swainsbury (on the left) with her Mary Quant hairstyle and Lois Ford, seen in the sixties. (Judy Hall collection)

(above) A 1961 two-tone pink and white Ford Consul Mk2. (Colin Caddy)

(below) A 1965 blue Ford Zephyr 4 Mk3. (Alan Hammond)

(above) The iconic sixties car, the Morris Mini, this one a 1961 Mk1 version. (Alan Hammond collection)

(below) Registered in 1952 is a Humber Hawk MkIV. (Eric Hammond)

(left) Kent Mod, Roger Curd, on his new Vespa 150GL in 1965, complete with parka. (Roger Curd collection)

(right) An eighties revival Mod, Bryn Owen, who was influenced by the Mod scene of the sixties. He is seen sitting on his Vespa 50 special. I'll let you count the mirrors and lights. (Bryn Owen collection) (right) Three original Bristol Mods looking cool in the early sixties. From left to right: Keith Price, Glyn Grainger and Reg Neate. (Glyn Grainger collection)

(below) Trouble outside Lloyds bank in Marlow. While the Rockers and the girls were in the Sugar Bowl café, the bank manager was annoyed that they had put their bikes in his parking space. So he piled the Enfield Crusader Sports, a BSA and the girls' bikes in a heap in the road. (Graham Hickman)

(left) Dover Saints Scooter Club outing in the summer of 1965, photographed in Market Square, Dover. (Roger Curd collection)

(below) A row of scooters on the approach road to Margate Station in the summer of 1964. (Roger Curd collection)

(above) The Fab Four – Paul, George, John and Ringo – photographed with Wilfrid Brambell on location at Minehead station while making the film A Hard Day's Night. (Mike Chilcott collection)

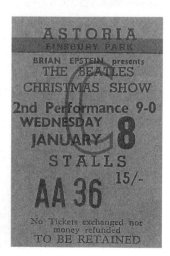

ASTORIA
FINSBURY PARK
BRIAN EPSTEIN presents
THE BEATLES
CHRISTMAS SHOW
2nd Performance 9-0
WEDNESDAY
JANUARY 8
STALLS
AA 36 15/-
No Tickets exchanged nor money refunded
TO BE RETAINED

(right) Ticket for seat AA36 at the Astoria Cinema in Finsbury Park, London, for The Beatles' Christmas show on 8 January 1964. (by courtesy of Eleanor Roberts)

(above) Shown in 1966 are the Minehead band The Witness 4. From left to right, Bill Hadley, lead guitar; Sid Court, bass guitar; Mike Herniman, drums; and Dave Pavling, rhythm guitar. (Chris Dyer collection)

REGAL BALLROOM, MINEHEAD

Chris Dyer presents

CLIFF BENNETT
AND THE
REBEL ROUSERS
WEDNESDAY, 23rd AUGUST, 1967, 8.30—12

ADMISSION 8/6

67

(left) A ticket for a gig by another sixties band, the Rebel Rousers. (Chris Dyer collection)

(above) Singer Herby Boxall with his sixties band, The Rockits, from Brighton. Note the rockets on the Goodman speakers which rest on top of a beer crate. (Herby Boxall collection)

(left) The well-known sixties band, The Blue Dukes, from Waltham-stow. Second from the right is guitarist Victor McCullough. (Victor McCullough collection)

(above) I played in an Essex band called Quota Plus, you must have heard of us?
From left to right, guitarist Dave Buthlay, guitarist Alan Hammond, singer Dave
Moore, drummer Brian Rowland and keyboard player Dave Hughes. (F.W. Tiler)

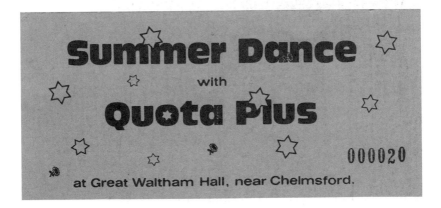

Alan Hammond, the bass guitarist with Quota Plus, shows off a fine line in tank-tops. (F.W. Tiler)

'You can say that again,' she said, not looking too impressed.

As she walked out of the door she gave us the evil eye. We agreed that we'd outstayed our welcome and it was time to do a runner. We finished off the food while Steve went for a jimmy riddle. A couple of minutes later he comes bursting in.

'We've been sussed, the management of the theatre and the group are heading this way. I was coming out of the bog and I could hear raised voices. The band's entourage will go garrety when they find out that we've eaten all the grub.'

It was too late to walk out of the door so we locked it from the inside and shot out of the window. We looked like The Lavender Hill Mob as we made our escape. We spent the rest of the afternoon relaxing on the beach, eating ice creams and studying the talent.

Using the free tickets, we had a great night at the theatre watching The ... , they were fantastic.

The next morning Mick phoned the B&B and told Tony that the management of the dance hall where we were playing had telexed him to say that all the tickets had been sold. But reality kicked in when Big Al said,

'Who's coming dog walking with me on the beach?'

I got the short straw, so after breakfast I went with him.

'Once he gets to know you, he'll be your mate for life,' Al said.

The dog had a massive chain attached to his collar which was the only way you could control him. To be fair, once he got to know me, he stopped growling and allowed me to stroke him. Everybody walking on the beach with their dogs gave us a wide berth as Big Al and Sampson looked a fearsome duo.

I got speaking to him about what he was up to; his life was his motorbike mates. Even at his young age he was the main face of their gang and that gave him a real edge. He'd just broken up with his girlfriend and was looking forward to sampling some of the talent on the tour. He'd sorted out his Rocker mates in advance to show him the sights at each of the venues. We wouldn't be seeing too much of him after the gigs.

By bringing Sampson he was able to do this; there's no way he was going to let the band down by having our gear nicked. We lit up two of his Player's Weights and let the dog off the chain for a run. We'd just had our last puff when, without warning, the dog eyed up a spaniel being walked by a girl of about our age. The spaniel didn't stand a chance as he tried to give it one; the poor dog was yelping, so was the owner. We rushed over and pulled him off the spaniel which was shivering with fright. The girl was crying and while Big Al controlled his dog, I apologised to her but she was not a happy bunny. After a bit of charm and once everything had calmed down, she lightened up. She caught the London accent and asked what I was doing in Bournemouth. When I told her our band was playing here she was delighted as she and her mate both had tickets for the gig. Her name was Dawn, and she lived locally. She wasn't bad, bit on the plump side, a fair looker and was blessed with a nice pair of Bristols. She had a Mary Quant hairdo, dead straight, with a fringe, and cut in a bob. I mentioned that maybe after the gig we could meet up with her. Then she let it slip that she was staying with her friend overnight whose parents were off to London to see a show, and didn't want to leave her on her own. It was getting better and better, and arrangements were made to see them later on.

That afternoon we went to the dance hall; there was no food laid on there. The hall was quite big and 300 people were booked in for the night. The manager was there to greet us; he looked a bit of a fly boy. I hope Mick gets paid for tonight, I thought. We didn't get involved with the money side of the business, as Mick had been straight down the line with us and our wages were being paid on time. But just in case, I introduced Big Al and Sampson to the hall owner and told him that he was our guarantee that we always got paid. Just then a few Rockers turned up to meet Al like a long-lost friend. The owner, seeing this crew turn up, went straight into his office and came out with a wad of cash for the night's gig, which he gave to Tony. Tony phoned Mick who was well happy. After that, we made a point of trying to get the money before or straight after the gig. Mick told us to pay the money into his business account, and to be fair, he upped the ante on our wages if we collected. The Rockers who turned up were diamonds, they helped us unload our gear and put it on stage for us. After we set up, Big Al went off with his mates, leaving the dog with us. He gave it a bone as big as a pig's head, which brought back memories of Ronnie. He said,

'As he knows you, you'll have to take him for a walk later.'

That would be fun. We did our soundcheck, in between a few friendly disagreements. The two sets were agreed, they were a mixture of covers and some of our own material. I told Steve we were sorted out for tonight on the crumpet front.

'What's she like?' he said all excited.

'I don't know, I haven't seen her.'

'Well, she could be a mutt?'

'You'll be all right then.'

Rick had sorted himself out a bird for tonight. He'd gone next door to a kiosk to get a packet of fags, and was served by a girl; after chatting her up he arranged to see her later. We were staying in the same B&B for two nights, as we were playing in Poole just up the coast the next night.

The four of us had dinner, then went and watched a classic war film in the afternoon, *The Great Escape*. Unfortunately, there was no Pathé News, which we used to like to watch when we were kids at Saturday morning pictures. We had our popcorn and a Jubbly. There was an art to eating a Jubbly. For the uninitiated, it was a triangular frozen orange drink that used to shoot across the floor if you squeezed its base too hard. To finish off, Tony rolled us all a liquorice paper filled with Old Holborn tobacco; that made us cough our lungs up.

We arrived back at the dance hall and it was starting to fill up. As we went in, who should be on the door, but the old boy with the thick-rimmed glasses from the theatre, and he wasn't happy.

'You four, you bloody well nearly lost me my job with your London spiv con tricks. The boss went mad when he realised you'd scoffed all the food and drink. He nearly called the police but luckily for you he didn't, I've a good mind to phone them myself right now.'

'Did your granddaughter and her mate enjoy the show last night?' asked Rick.

He went a bit quiet, realising they had two dodgy tickets. He calmed down and we apologised and bought him a brown ale. In the end he was as good as gold and even laughed when we asked him why there was no grub in our dressing room.

It was a large dance hall with plenty of space for dancing. There was a nice bar there and I went and brought back a tray of light ales.

In our two sets we included 'For Your Love' by The Yardbirds; 'I Can't Explain' and 'Anyway, Anyhow, Anywhere' by The Who; 'Baby Please Don't Go' by Them; and some Stones and Beatles numbers. We'd put together eight of our own numbers, including a few songs which we really felt had some potential. We did our final soundcheck and we were ready to party.

The hall was full and we were up for it. Anyone who's played in a group will know the great feeling of playing live to an audience, it's magic. There you are, 18 years of age, on tour with your mates, playing to full houses across the south-west of England. The curtain went across and we launched straight into 'All Day and All of the Night' by The Kinks. There was a good response to the first number and it got better as the night went on. It doesn't always happen, as we'd find out later. The adrenalin was pumping and sweat was pouring off us as we finished the first set. We went back into our dressing room to have a few beers. The second set would be mostly our own numbers. Big Al had pulled a Rocker girl who was wearing tight leathers, well tasty. Rick's kiosk girl was there, she was a Dutch student. Half way through our break there was a knock on the door. Dawn from the beach was standing there wearing a pink see-through, crocheted dress and a velvet cap. There was nothing left to the imagination, it was all on show, and I couldn't wait for the gig to finish. Steve was all eyes and licking his lips at the thought of his blind date. She came in too, well, two of her came in. She was a size and looked like she could eat for Bournemouth. Steve's face was a picture as Dawn introduced her friend Bertha to him. Steve nodded, he wasn't impressed. She did have a nice personality and offered him a Player's No 6, which he took. The buzzer went and we were on again. Dawn and Bertha said they'd meet us by our van when the gig finished. They made it quite clear that there was plenty of drink back at the house. After the girls went, Steve took a few wind-ups from the other lads.

'It'll take you an hour to find it in the creases,' Tony said.

Rick then said, 'Let us know where you're staying tonight, Steve, because the size of her, we'll probably need a JCB to get you out.'

'Bollocks,' said Steve. 'Leave me out tonight, Nick; you can have both of them. Bertha's not for me, she'd kill me if she sat on top of me, and she's got tits like a Jersey cow.'

'It'll be a right laugh; free booze and she isn't that bad.'

'Leave it out, she's grim.'

'That's not very nice, she someone's daughter.'

'Oh, piss off.'

We were both winding each other up as we went back on stage to start the second set, which was tiptop. We played the final number and walked off. If the audience has enjoyed your music, you wait for the clapping and cheering for an encore, which in the music business is called 'a false tab'. We weren't disappointed, they called out for more. We went back out there for another two numbers and finished the evening well happy. I convinced Steve that free drinks and a few laughs with the two girls was a good way to finish off; he wasn't convinced but he went along with it.

With no roadies, it was all hands to the pumps to get the gear safely packed away. Big Al and a couple of his biker mates worked like Trojans, and within a short time everything was in and we were ready to go. He took the van back to the digs plus our guitars; these were never left in the van overnight.

We'd just finished when the two girls turned up. As soon as they clocked us they grabbed our hands and marched us to Bertha's house just around the corner. Bertha held Steve's hand in a vice-like grip; she wasn't going to let her prey go. Dawn was gentler, in fact I quite liked her. It did help that she had a nice pair. The house was really upmarket, there was definitely a few bob in the family. Steve's eyes lit up when he saw the drinks cabinet; within a few minutes the lights were low, the Dansette was playing 'True Love Ways' by Peter and Gordon, and drinks were flowing. Me and Steve had a couple of bottles of Blue Nun between us, the first time we'd tasted wine. It went down well with a Long John whisky chaser. The girls were drinking barley wine, which was a powerful drink. It was all slow music and the dancing was close and intimate. The wine was hitting the spot, as Steve thought he was dancing with actress Jane Asher and he was Paul McCartney. The next thing I knew Bertha had whipped Steve upstairs. He'd put up a bit of a fight, but was now on Booth's Gin, and was anybody's. Bertha had her man and there's no way she was going to release him. Dawn and I sort of drifted upstairs to Sandie Shaw's 'I'll Stop at Nothing'. Unfortunately, the needle got stuck on this record and kept playing it over and over again.

About an hour later there was a shout from Bertha,

'Bleedin' hell, my mum and dad are back, you've got to get out of here now, they'll kill me.'

When you're half drunk with hardly any clothes on and can't get downstairs, there's a problem. Bertha came into the room like a mad bull, and man-handled me into her room which faced the back garden; Dawn followed. Bertha opened the window and told us both to jump out. We weren't that pissed that we were going to jump 30 feet into her back garden.

'There's a ledge outside the window,' said Bertha. 'You can shimmy down the drain pipe, it's only just a few feet from the ground. After that, you can jump the rest.'

'Do I look simple?' Steve said, 'I hate heights.'

The decision was made for us when her dad came in the front door and shouted out,

'Are you still awake, darling?'

We climbed out of the window with just our trousers on. There we were on the ledge like a couple of window cleaners. The window slammed behind us, the light was switched off and we were on our own, in the dark.

'Another fine mess you've got me into, Stanley', said Steve (Stan of Laurel and Hardy fame).

We curled up laughing and couldn't stop ourselves. We soon livened up when a gust of wind nearly tipped us over the edge. We somehow found the drainpipe and me being brave or stupid slid down it first, and then jumped the last few feet. Next thing I know, I'm gasping for breath. I've jumped straight into a bleedin' great fish pond as deep as a lake. I'm like a drowned rat. Steve's bottle went when he heard the shouting coming from the house, he jumps and joins me in the fish pond.

'Why didn't you tell me, you jodrell? I'm soaked through.'

With a couple of goldfish for company, we made our way back to the digs, fortunately not far away. One problem. It was two in the morning, we'd no key, we were dripping water everywhere and cold. Steve looked at me and I knew what was coming next.

'No way am I sleeping in that van with that bloody great dog.'

Then it started to rain. So I knocked on the back of the Commer and he sprang into action, putting his giant nose to the window. He started barking and baring its teeth but as soon as he saw me he stopped. I unlocked the back of the van and he jumped out and went and cocked his leg. He didn't want to get wet either and jumped back into his warm bed. Steve went up front and lay across the front seat while I had the dog and Vox amps for company all night. Me and Steve were both whacked out and fell asleep virtually straight away. Mind you, I'd one eye open for the dog, I didn't want to be ravished by him. The thing snored and farted all night.

We were woken by Big Al who laughed when he saw us both in the van, especially me curled up with his dog. We had a late breakfast and went over the previous night and our evening's entertainment. Big Al had come back early, as he was a bit worried about leaving the gear overnight for the first time, which was well decent of him. He was seeing his biker girl again tonight in Poole and was going to make up for lost time. Rick went back to his girl's flat and discussed how the Dutch and English could work closer together. Tony had found a milk bar open. A couple of girls recognised him as the drummer in the band they'd just seen and he was bought free espressos all night. He wouldn't say but I think he had more than a coffee. We all agreed that the gig went down well. We were just about to leave when Bertha and Dawn turned up with two carrier bags. They'd tracked us down, then Bertha told us about her mum and dad coming back early.

'There were problems with the trains to London, so my parents had a meal in Bournemouth with their friends and came back to the house.'

Even with all the commotion, all they got was a bollocking for drinking her parents' booze. They never sussed out we'd been round there. We got up to go when Dawn handed me a bag with some of my clothes in. Rick looked closely in the bag.

'Christ, look at those striped pants,' he said. 'Talk about a Tiger in your tank.'

He took another look at the bag and said,

'I don't believe it, there's all skid marks on them.'

We took the bags off the girls and had a final snog. They gave us their phone numbers to keep in touch. Bertha had left her mark on Steve, with the biggest love bite I'd ever seen. I reckoned she'd used one of those rubber plungers that you stick in the sink when it's blocked. In fact it was there all the way through the tour as a memory of Bournemouth.

♫ 16 ♫

Burnham-on-Sea & Scrumpy

After Poole, we played the Isle of Wight, Portsmouth, South-
ampton and Winchester, before going on to various gigs in
Somerset, Devon and Cornwall. Mick kept in contact with
us all the time, and the feedback he'd got from the venues was
positive; they wanted to re-book us if we toured the south-
west again. Now, we had a little bit of a result. *Music Scene*
was the main national musical paper. We'd actually got a small
mention as an up-and-coming Mod band that was on tour in
the south-west and well worth going to see.

With Big Al in touch with the local Rocker fraternities,
they'd come out in their droves to see him at our gigs. He said
they were our extra security if needed – doesn't make sense,
does it? We were a Mod group, and Rockers were helping us.
Of course without him that wouldn't have happened and we'd
have been fair game for a good hiding.

We played our first gig in the west country at Burnham-
on-Sea in Somerset; we were then off to Taunton, Minehead
and Bridgwater. This B&B turned out to be the best one we
stayed at on the whole tour; we were well pleased we were here
for two nights. We arrived at Burnham the night before, giving
us a free evening. Moira, the landlady, was a good looker, about
30 years old, which in our young eyes was middle-aged. Her
husband was in the Merchant Navy, so she was maybe a bit
lonely. She took an instant shine to Rick, as all the women did,
and liked the idea of an Essex touring band staying at her place.
We could usually only afford breakfast, the rest of the time we

snacked out on whatever we could get hold of. She cooked us a nice meal that evening. In fact our stay there cost us next to nothing, more of that later. We were cream-crackered and wanted a quiet evening so after the meal we watched *Bonanza* on the old television, and then went our separate ways. A good idea, as living in each other's pockets can cause a bit of aggro. To be fair though, we hardly ever fell out with each other.

Tony wanted to go and see Glastonbury Tor which was about 10 miles away, so he had the motor. For the uninitiated, the Tor is a teardrop-shaped hill with ruins on top, featuring the roofless St Michael's Tower. Tor is a local word of Celtic origin meaning conical hill; it also has mythological characters of the supernatural attached to it. In other words, you've got be potty to walk up a steep hill to see a roofless building. I'm sure Tony was hoping to meet a Druid and enjoy a meaningful evening with somebody from the other side.

Rick was having a quiet night in with our landlady, who made it quite clear that she was on her own tonight and would love to have some company. I'd wondered why she never charged us for the evening meal.

Me and Steve decided to walk around the corner to a real old Somerset pub and mix with the natives. A few hundred yards up the road was *The Smugglers' Inn*. We went in and sat down near some old boys who were enjoying their pint of scrumpy and a game of dominoes. When we went to order our beers, our London accent was picked up straight away. The average age in the pub was about 70, so two 18-year-olds from London way was a bit of a novelty. One of the old boys said,

'What you doing down this way, lads?'

We told him about our gig the next night. We were well surprised that he knew all about it and so did the rest of the pub.

'It's a big event for the town,' he said, 'and it's making headline news for all the youngsters in the area. The place will be packed out so you give them a good night.'

We were quite chuffed about that and he invited us to sit with him and five other old-timers. Claude was doing most of the talking.

'We don't like all this new pop music,' he said. 'We prefer the songs of Adge Cutler.' (Adge Cutler later formed The Wurzels in 1966 and had those classic numbers 'Drink Up Thy Zider' and 'The Combine Harvester'. He sadly died in 1974, but The Wurzels are still going strong.)

They were all drinking the local scrumpy, it looked evil and there was no way we were going to drink it. Scrumpy is very strong cider and after one pint, the world begins to glow; a second glass makes it disappear; and with a third glass you're in orbit. Claude let me have a sip of his; it was horrible so we stuck to our light and bitters. We found out during the conversation that they were ex-lifeboat men. It doesn't matter what age you are, sex comes into the conversation. Old Claude said to us,

'Bet you two are getting plenty of it from your travels around the country.' Then he continued, 'We've all had our moments. Take old Jake for instance.'

Jake was about 80, he had a mop of white hair, a long white beard and was smoking from an old clay pipe. Another six pints of pure scrumpy was ordered and we had a couple more light and bitters, and treated ourselves to some Percy Dalton peanuts. Pipes were filled and roll-ups were made and the story was about to be told by Claude on Jake's behalf.

'It was Jake's first dabble with the opposite sex,' he said. 'It was a Sunday afternoon and he'd been courting this local girl called, Maud, for about three months. She came from a strict

Baptist family and sex was strictly taboo before marriage. They'd been to Chapel on the Sunday morning, and as it was a nice sunny afternoon he took her for a walk along the beach.'

The old boys at the table started laughing, and put Claude off his stroke. He continued,

'Jake slipped his hand into Maud's and he walked to the end of the beach over to a sand dune, well away from prying eyes. He had these big baggy trousers on, which hid his evil thoughts. Jake was thinking to himself how could he get Maud into the sand dune? Maud was a strapping girl and her father was the local Baptist minister, so God had to play a roll. As he neared the dune he said to Maud, "Shall we pray to God for this wonderful day?" They got to the dune, knelt down and prayed to the almighty. Jake couldn't stand it anymore and grabbed hold of her and starting kissing her all over. "Maud, Maud, I want you," he said. The passion had taken over and Jake couldn't control himself.'

'Think of God, think of God. He wouldn't approve,' said Maud.

'But he's not here,' replied Jake.

'Jake couldn't get his trousers off so he gets his fishing knife out of the side of his trousers and cuts the cord. They dropped to the ground and Jake was ready for action.'

Claude pauses and said, 'I need a refill,' so the scrumpy round was ordered again. Jake was sweating like a pig; he was reliving the moment, and it gave him time to fill up his pipe with a large portion of Bondman tobacco.

'Right,' said Claude, 'where was I? Yes, well, Maud wasn't shouting out anymore, and God wasn't being mentioned. Then Jake couldn't believe his luck.'

'Take me, Jake, take me,' Maud shouted.

'I will, I will,' replied Jake.

'They were all over each other, and going at it hammer and tongs. Jake was at the ready and he went for it. His first sexual conquest and he couldn't wait. He'd just entered paradise, when God got his own back. Rockets went up in the air to launch the lifeboat. A lifeboat crew is trained to stop whatever they're doing, and get to the lifeboat station at all costs. Jake was no exception to the rule. He had one final thrust, yanked up his trousers and ran to the lifeboat station, which was a few hundred yards away. Poor old Jake, his moment of heaven had gone. When he got there it was a false alarm but the damage had been done.'

'What damage?' I said to Claude.

'Well, Billy, our pub landlord, was their end product. Jake and Maud are his mum and dad.'

The whole pub erupted with laughter, including Billy. The tale had been told many times, but it was still funny. We had a great night with the old boys and we promised that if we were this way again we'd definitely pop in and see them.

Next morning we had a long lay-in. The landlady had a twinkle in her eye and an extra spring to her step, thanks to Rick, who looked worn out. He wouldn't go into the details, but 30-year-old women were definitely for him. Tony wasn't up, so he was probably having a lay-in as well. Rick, who he roomed with had obviously put his head down elsewhere last night, and had even moved his clothes into the landlady's room, so Tony had the room to himself.

'Moira, have you seen Tony?' asked Rick.

'No, his bed's still made up.'

Alarm bells were just starting to ring because Tony was never late. I went upstairs and as Moira had said, the bed had not been slept in. Steve went round to the back of the house and only the van was there. So there was no Tony and no motor.

As luck would have it the gig wasn't far away, so Big Al drove the van and we walked to the hall. The owner was there and he got one of his staff to make us some tea while we unloaded.

'This is one of the biggest dances I've held in Burnham,' he said, 'and I've sold all the tickets. There are people coming from all over Somerset.'

We still couldn't fathom Tony's non-appearance. He was one of those guys who'd never let you down. So we had no drummer at the hall, the fuses kept blowing when we switched our amps on, and we were playing in five hours' time. Steve went to ring Mick to see whether Tony had been in contact with him. A couple of minutes later he was back and said,

'Do you want the good news or the bad news first?'

'Just hit us with it,' I said.

'The good news is that somebody from one of the major record companies in the country is coming to see us play tonight. One of their big groups was playing in Bristol last night, they stayed overnight and they're coming to see us play. Mick was supposed to be coming tonight but his mum's had a heart attack and it's touch and go whether she's going to make it, so we're on our own. And no, he hasn't heard from Tony. Before I could say anything he asked why Tony hadn't rung him this morning as he normally did. I didn't have the heart to tell him he'd gone AWOL.'

Moira walked into the dance hall, could see we all had the hump, and asked why. On hearing our problems, she asked,

'Have you been in touch with the local hospitals or police in case he's had an accident?'

Being selfish bastards we hadn't thought of that. We were more concerned that we didn't have a drummer for the most important gig of our lives.

'Leave it to me,' she said, 'I'll phone around and come back to you.'

The owner came over to us, he looked a bit concerned.

'Is everything alright lads, you seem a bit worried, there's not a problem about tonight?'

'Course not, guv,' said Rick, 'Everything's as sweet as a nut. Is there any more Brooke Bond in the pot and any more of them Kit Kats to go with it?'

It was now 3.30, and members of the manager's team were arriving to set the hall up ready for the night. There was even a queue forming outside. Moira came back; the good news was that there'd been no reported accidents.

'Perhaps one of the druids at the Tor has whipped him away to Stonehenge,' Steve said, which brought a few titters.

None of us could play drums and you've got to have a drummer.

'We'll have to cancel if he doesn't show,' I said.

Nobody said anything.

Then Moira, who I was starting to like, said,

'Can't you find another drummer?'

Without going into the ins and outs of drumming, to find another drummer in four hours who could play all our numbers was near enough an impossibility. We had to face up to it, we were in deep trouble.

'I thought you Essex boys were made of sterner stuff. You can't give up now,' said Moira.

I was now going off her. She knew as much about music as I did about sewing.

'There's a music shop just outside Burnham, and I know the guys in there, we went to the same school; they might know somebody,' she said.

We ignored her comments. Steve looked out of the window.

'Christ, this queue is getting longer and longer,' he said. 'We're going to have to do something soon. We can't sit here like spare pricks at a wedding.'

'There's going to be a riot if you don't play tonight,' said Big Al. 'The first thing that'll go is your equipment; they'll kick it all over the hall and then you'll be next.'

'You're right,' I said.

So Moira, Big Al and myself went to the music shop. We left the dog with Steve and Rick who carried on getting as much set up on stage as possible.

Before we walked into the shop, Big Al stopped to admire a gleaming motorbike outside, which he said was an Ariel 1000cc, four-cylinder, with twin crankshafts; they cost a fortune. I was well impressed but it didn't help us get a drummer. I walked in with Moira who was greeted like a long lost friend, they seemed nice guys. I told them our problems; in fact they were coming tonight. One of them, Ritchie, said,

'There aren't too many drummers around here who could do what you want. There's one guy, Denny, who I happen to know well. He could do it for you. He works at our other music shop in Bristol. The only problem is he's just smashed his car up and hasn't got transport, and whether he'd do it is another story.'

'Could you give him a bell for us?' I asked.

'Of course.'

He rang the other shop. Denny was having his tea break. 'He'll ring back in a minute,' said Ritchie.

What a time to have a tea break, I'm saying to myself, with only three and a half hours before we've got to play. To be fair, he rang back within a couple of minutes. Ritchie had a word with him and passed the phone to me. I explained our problem. (In fact he'd read about us in *Music Scene*. I found out later that the lovely Diane's brother, Pete, was the journalist who had written the article about us. He'd got in touch with Mick and he had given him the lowdown on us.) I went through the material we were playing. Denny sounded drugged up to me, he was definitely on something. I couldn't seem to get through to him. In the corner of my eye I could see Big Al having a strong chat with Ritchie and pointing outside. Suddenly he grabbed the phone and said to Denny,

'Look mate, we need you, I'll be picking you up within the hour. It's a great gig and a great band and I'm told you're the best drummer in Bristol. What do you say? Right, I'm on my way; I'll be with you within the hour.'

Ritchie hands Big Al a key, and a business card with an address on it, and he rushes out of the shop.

'I've got to be bleedin' mad. I've only known you lot five minutes and I've lent your mate my Ariel 1000cc to pick up Denny.'

It was all going too fast for me, so I sat down and lit up a Woodbine.

'We do appreciate all your help, Ritchie, but I've got one final favour to ask,' I said.

'You can have the shop,' he said, and throws me the keys. We all burst out laughing.

'What else do you want?'

'We've got a problem with a couple of the amps; have you got anybody who can have a look at them?'

He took the keys back and gave them to his mate and told him to lock up, as he was coming with us to have a look at these amps, and said he would see him later at the gig. The three of us jumped in the van to go back to the hall. Then Ritchie said,

'I don't know if your mate is going to get to the gig on time, he's going to pick-up the Friday rush-hour traffic out of Bristol.'

That's all I wanted to hear. I just blanked him; I was in no mood to take that on board. I'm thinking to myself, I've only been in Somerset 24 hours and I've sat with six old boys, hammered out of their brains listening to Jake's first bunk-up in the sand dunes; Tony's disappeared off the face of the earth, probably in some coven with a load of weirdos; I'm driving a Commer van, with a randy landlady and some poor sod who's lent his prize motorbike to a mad Rocker, who's probably knocking the bollocks out of it right now; and if he does find the drummer, and gets him to ride pillion, he'll be a mental wreck and in no fit state to play drums, and with a band he's never played with before. Oh yeah, and I've just run out of Woodbines.

When we got there, Steve and Rick had done a great job getting everything in place on the stage, and they had even got the drums set up. I told them about the developments and they just worked on. The edgy owner came up on stage to make sure everything was on track, as he hadn't heard a soundcheck. We told him to keep out of the way as we were busy. Ritchie had found the fault with the amps, which was just a couple of loose connections. We had some kind of soundcheck, and now we were in Big Al's hands. Moira went back home to see if Tony had rung – he hadn't. With 45 minutes to go and the place packed to the rafters, Big Al has done the business. He ran in with a shaking, dishevelled Denny, who then lit up a joint and said,

'Somebody get me a bleedin' scotch and a purple heart. That bloke's a nutter. I've had my eyes closed all the way from Bristol. He's been weaving in and out of the traffic at 100 miles an hour. I'm sure he must have thought he was racing the TT circuit on the Isle of Man.'

Now he'd got that out of his system, it was back to the job in hand. Denny was about 23, with long hair down to his shoulders and a droopy moustache. There was more fat on a pork chop than on him. I reckoned the drugs were having an effect on him, as he had the shakes. He'd played for various bands in and around Bristol and was doing some session work. Denny went straight to the drums and was well impressed with the Ludwig kit. We went through the two sets we were playing. He knew quite a few of the numbers, but of course none of our own material. We had a couple of numbers which we thought were pretty good. We had to play them tonight because the record guy was coming. So we went through the songs with him as best we could.

We were ready to go, Moira and Ritchie moved off the stage and it was now or never. I saw Denny pop a couple of pills, they looked like Blues, but that was none of my business. If it made him play the drums better, so be it. Normally we'd go straight into the number when we first started, but tonight we felt we needed to get the audience on our side first, because of the problems we'd had. The curtain was pulled and charmer Rick went into his patter before we played the music and bent the truth a bit.

'It's a pleasure to be in Burnham-on-Sea tonight and it's great to see so many people here. Tony our drummer has had to rush back to Essex to see his mother as she's had a suspected heart attack. There's no way we could let you down tonight, Burnham, so at very short notice, Denny, one of your guys has come to our rescue.'

Denny stood up and the cheers echoed around the hall.

'Right, let's have a great night, Burnham.'

Rick looked at me and we went straight into 'Don't Bring Me Down' by The Pretty Things. I have to say Denny saved the show; he was a real pro. We had a few cock-ups but overall it was a great night. Our own 'Suburban Mod', went down really well with the boys and girls of Burnham. Whether the guy from the record company liked what he heard, we'd find out later.

After the euphoria of the night before, reality kicked in at breakfast as Tony had still not shown. We were going to have to tell Mick and maybe get in touch with the police. Denny had said that he could do the Taunton gig tonight, but we had to let him know by eleven o'clock this morning. With the amount of drugs Denny was popping last night we wondered if he'd still be alive by then.

I was just dipping the last soldier into my boiled egg when there was a loud knock on the door. A few seconds later Tony came into the room looking like a bag of shit.

'I'm really sorry, guys,' he said, 'I've let you down. I've been to hell and back. Is there a cup of Rosie available?'

Moira poured him a cup of tea.

'Do you want a cooked breakfast?' Moira asked.

'Thanks, but I couldn't face anything right now.'

We were, of course, pleased to see him back but annoyed he'd let us down. He downed his tea in one gulp and mother hen filled it up for him again.

'What's the SP then, Tony?' Rick said. 'We've got another gig tonight, and you look like you couldn't play with yourself, let alone a set of drums.'

'You know I went to Glastonbury Tor, what a great place that is, do you know there is ...'

'Cut out the Hans Christian Andersen crap,' said an annoyed Steve. 'Get to the point.'

'At the top of the Tor there were these two girls. After we'd seen the sights and watched the sun go down we went and had a drink with some of their friends. We went to a flat in Glastonbury and took a couple of barrels of the local scrumpy. You know I do like a Cox's apple and this brew has a real apple taste, and it slid down well. It was nectar.'

'How many glasses did you have?' inquired Moira.

'It's hard to say, but whatever is in a small barrel.'

'A barrel! That's about eight pints. You should be dead by now.'

'I think I am, Moira. After the last glass I just went into orbit, and woke up this morning in bed with the two girls, and a head like an atom bomb.'

'That sounds really terrible waking up in bed with two girls. My heart bleeds for you,' said a jealous Rick.

'Forget that, can you play tonight?' I asked.

'I hope so,' he said.

We bought Moira some flowers (paid for and not from the local park) and settled up the bill, which was peanuts compared with what she gave us in return. I think we had to thank Rick for that. After the Taunton gig, Rick went back to Moira's in the Consul for a night of passion, and we drove on to Minehead in the van where we were playing the next day. We met Rick the next morning and he had a smile on his face like the cat that got the cream.

We never told Mick about Tony's love affair with scrumpy, and unfortunately, we never heard from the record company, which was a real downer. Mick still couldn't join the tour, as his mum remained dangerously ill. We finally finished the Somerset part of the tour by playing Yeovil. We took the opportunity to watch Yeovil Town football club play on their famous sloping pitch, always worth a goal start for the home team.

♫ 17 ♫

Exeter & Miniskirts

From Somerset we moved on to Devon and Cornwall. 1965 was the era of the miniskirt. Fashion designers Mary Quant, John Bates and André Courrèges were all responsible for raising the hemline and there's an argument as to who invented it first. We blokes didn't care, we just enjoyed it. Of course, then came the micro skirt. As one magazine stated,

'It covers not much more than the intimate parts.'

We were playing Exeter for two nights and then on down to the Devon coast. We had a day off; Rick drove back to Burnham in the Consul to see Moira, Tony just wanted to sleep in his room, as he was still getting over scrumpy poisoning. The rest of us and the animal fancied a day at the seaside so we went to Dawlish in the van. The B&B owner allowed us to store our equipment in one of his spare rooms. So off we went down to the Devon coast. We acted like kids, playing the slot machines and having Lyons Maid orange lollies. Next stop the Del Rio coffee bar, and we had large frothy coffees with two sugar lumps, and a knickerbocker glory each. They had a Wurlitzer jukebox and I picked out 'I'm Telling You Now' by Freddie & The Dreamers, 'Catch the Wind' by Donovan and Sandie Shaw's 'Long Live Love'.

My hair was long and in a mess and I badly needed a haircut, so off I went to the nearest hairdressers, while the others did their own thing. I walked in, it was a ladies and gents combined salon, which was unusual. A girl slightly older than me had just finished this old biddy's hair.

'I'll be with you in a minute,' she said, as the old girl gave her a 2/6d tip. Christ, I could live like a king for a day on that. The old girl went out of the door and the hairdresser came over to me.

'Unfortunately, the barber's gone sick.'

So I started to walk out.

'I could do it if you want me to?'

She saw my expression as I pooh-poohed her suggestion.

'Suit yourself,' she said.

At this time women hardly ever cut men's hair, which brings me to a funny story that one of our mates John, told us. This bloke, like me, goes into a hairdressers and has a girl cut his hair for the first time. The hairdresser puts the sheet around him to begin the cut. He takes his glasses off, and puts his hands together with the glasses underneath the sheet. She's just finished cutting his hair when she sees some activity going on under the sheet. She observes this and goes mad; she picks up her metal hairdryer and clumps him across the head with it. She then rushes out of the shop, calling him a dirty old bastard, and says she's going to call the police. This girl thinks he's playing with himself underneath it, but all he was doing was cleaning his glasses with the sheet.

I didn't want to wander the streets looking for a barber on my day off so I said, 'Okay.'

'Now, you're sure?' she said.

I apologised and sat in the chair while she put the sheet around me. I made sure my hands were in full view!

'How'd you want it cut?'

'Just a trim with a Boston,' I said. She put her hands on my head and there was an instant tingle, her touch was magic. I went straight from a trim to 'Can you wash it first, please?'

'Of course,' she said, 'come over to the wash basin.'

When I was younger and mum used to wash my hair, I used to kneel on a chair and put my head over the sink, and this is what I did. She fell about laughing.

'What are you doing?' she said.

'Getting my hair washed,' I replied.

'Not like that. Sit down and lean your head back over the sink and I'll do the rest.'

There's me thinking, I'm supposed to be the dog's bollocks from Essex and she's this country girl with rosy cheeks and knows nothing. Did I feel a wally. She started washing my hair, it was giving me goose pimples.

'What's your name?'

'Anita.'

She was putting on this expensive Vidal Sassoon shampoo. It was better than the Sunlight soap or Squezy washing-up liquid we used at home. The sensation from her hands made me want more.

'You couldn't give it an extra rinse, Anita, I haven't washed it for well over two weeks.'

'What? That's not very hygienic, is it?'

She went and put a pair of lightweight gloves on and gave it a final rinse. She sat me back in the chair, took the gloves off, put them straight in the bin, and started cutting my hair.

'You're not from around here, are you on holiday?'

'No, I'm working here for two days.'

'What do you do then?'

I gave it the big one and said,

'I play lead guitar in a group and we're playing a big gig in Exeter tomorrow night.'

'Oh.'

Is that all I was worth, an 'oh'?, I said to myself. She then started laughing.

'It's horrible when there's a lack of interest, isn't it?'

She was going back to when I first walked in and blanked her about cutting my hair. I was starting to like her. She had a great sense of humour and I was hoping the haircut was going to last all day. Then she said.

'What's your name, then?'

'Nick.'

I looked at her in the mirror. She was about 19 with a bee-hive hairdo and quite nice looking. She wore a red hipster mini-skirt and a white skinny rib top. I added a new perfume to my list – I asked her what she was wearing, as it smelt beautiful.

'Secret de Venus,' she replied.

I was still dreaming when she said, 'All finished.' I got up and was well pleased with what she'd done. I paid her the four bob and a tanner tip which I could see she wasn't too impressed with. She went to the door and put the closed sign up.

'Look,' I said, 'I feel a bit mean about the tip, can I buy you a coffee and maybe something to eat?'

'I don't think so,' she replied.

'Sorry if I've annoyed you.'

'No, it's not that, it's, just, well I don't know you and I was going to eat my sandwiches in the park.'

'I just thought that there's a nice coffee bar a few doors away; they've got tables outside, the sun's shining and I'd love to have a coffee with you.'

'You're a bit forward, aren't you?'

'Hey, just a coffee and a chat. By the way, what's in the sarnies? I'm feeling a bit peckish.'

'You're full of yourself, ain't you,' she replied.

'I suppose I am, just the coffee then?'

'The sandwiches are ham salad,' she said with a smile.

'Have they got any Pan Yan pickle in them?'

She laughed and said, 'Just a quick coffee, then.'

I took her to the coffee bar and we got a table outside overlooking the beach. I got the coffees in and she shared her sandwiches with me. She was lovely and we had a good laugh, until she told me she was engaged.

'How long?' I asked.

'About a year,' she said.

She hardly asked about the band. Normally when you say you're in a band, girls get a little bit excited but not her. We were having a great chat and a laugh. She didn't own the shop, she was just running it while her boss was away.

ॐ ॐ ॐ

I'm as happy as Larry, as they say. Then out of the corner of my eye I see this four-wheeler bike, you know, one of those fun ones you see at the seaside. Sitting on the bike are Big Al, Steve and the dog, all wearing kiss-me-quick hats, even the dog had one on. Steve's ringing the bell loudly and scoffing candy floss. Everyone is looking at them and giving them a wide berth. They pass by where we're sitting, and I duck down, so they don't see me. I think it's worked, until the dog spots me, jumps off and bounds towards me. He jumps all over me, nearly knocking me off the chair, and smothers me with licks, then the other two spot me. Anita can't believe what's happening, her mouth is wide open. She'd said that she'd never been to London, and after meeting this lot, she's probably thinking she's done herself a favour not going.

'Who's the sort then, Nick?' asks Steve.

'Steve, come on, leave the love birds alone. Let's go for another ride,' says Big Al.

He can see I want to be left alone, so he pulls the dog back onto the bike. But not Steve, he's eyeing up Anita.

'On your bike,' I say, 'I'll see you later.'

He takes the hint, but has to have the last word as he's pulling away, and ringing the bell madly.

'Give her one for me, Nick, will yer?'

They are off up the road, almost colliding with a Hillman Imp, and then it all goes quiet. Anita's eyes follow them, she looks at me bemused, then bursts out laughing.

'What planet have you lot come from?'

There isn't a lot I can say.

'Are they close friends of yours?' she says, still laughing.

I try to explain who they are, but I think it goes over her head. She says it's time to open up again. I walk back to the shop with her and I don't really know what to say. She unlocks the shop door, turns around and faces me.

'It was nice to meet you, Nick, and I wish you all the best with tomorrow's show.'

'You're really nice, Anita, and I wish ... '

Then the phone in the salon starts to ring.

'You wish what?'

'I wish ... '

Just then a woman pushes past me into the shop, and shuts the door in my face while Anita goes to answer the phone and that's the end of that.

ॐ ॐ ॐ

I wasn't happy with Steve when I met him later on, especially his one-liner about Anita; in fact I went into one, the first time that me and Steve had fallen out since Vicky and the pyorrhoea joke.

'You sound like bleedin' Mary Whitehouse,' he said.

I must have got it bad with Anita to carry on like this. Steve was in one of those annoying moods all day.

We were driving back to our digs, Steve was at the wheel. The miniskirts were outrageous, indecent, thank goodness. Being blokes, we were trying to see if you could see their knickers as they walked by or bent over. The best girl I ever saw wearing a miniskirt was model Jean Shrimpton. We had a mate who was a bus conductor and when he saw a bird with a miniskirt get on his bus he'd stand in their way and say, 'Sorry luv, room upstairs only.' Of course as they went up the stairs he followed their move on the highly polished mirror. I always wondered why he had that duster in his back pocket.

We got lost going back to our digs and he'd ended up in the main street of the town. Because we were driving around in the Commer van with the name of the band stamped all over it, we were getting plenty of attention from the girls. These two tasty blondes were walking on the driver's side. Steve looked to the right and said,

'Look at those two. They've got red knickers on, I do like red knickers.'

'Look out Steve!' I said, too late.

We'd hit a motor up the arse. Thankfully Steve was quick on the brake, so it was only a tap. I glanced at the car.

'Oh, no, you've hit a Ford Anglia and it's only a police car with two young coppers in it.'

The two coppers got out of their car with notebooks in their hands. I got out of the van with Steve and sheepishly looked at the two vehicles. Fortunately, there was no damage. Then Steve said to one of the coppers in a sincere voice,

'What can I say, sir? I'm in the wrong and all I can do is apologise.'

The coppers were expecting maybe a bit of verbal from us but what can you say when you're banged to rights. The two coppers inspected the van and were surprised that it was in such good condition and with all the relevant paper work up-to-date. As soon as they saw 'Modern Edge' on the side, they were much friendlier. One of them asked,

'Are you the band that's playing in town tomorrow?'

'That's us,' I replied. The other one said,

'We've been trying to get a couple of tickets for your show.'

We'd kept Big Al out of sight, as he looked like a thug, especially as he hadn't shaved for a week. Suddenly a hand with two tickets appeared out of the van, which I grabbed. For whatever reason, the manager of this venue had sent us some free tickets.

'Well, have two tickets on us.'

He looked at them and then at his mate and I thought I've dropped one here. He's going to do me for bribing a police officer. The copper took them from my hand and said,

'As there's no damage, take this as a warning.'

As they were getting back in to their police car, the other one said,

'This had better be the best gig you've ever played.'

That night we all went to the pictures to see Sean Connery play James Bond in *From Russia With Love*, except Rick who went back down to Burnham to see Moira. Afterwards we went on to a nightclub and met up with some girls who were out on a hen night from Exmouth. They really let their hair down. It was a great night and morning, and it was definitely one to remember.

After only two hours sleep, we had to get to the venue where we were playing. We all felt some practice was needed on some of our own numbers, which we were introducing more and more into the sets. We'd phoned the venue the previous day to make sure we could get in early, so we loaded up and off we went. When we arrived there, something wasn't quite right. Plastered on the windows were posters of our band, which was great. Mick had got some photos taken of us and sent them to the various gigs we were playing at. I didn't say anything to the others as we got out of the van, but I could see they were thinking the same as me. Big Al took the van around the back to unload. We were greeted warmly by the manager and he said,

'I'll send a couple of my lads around the back to help your crew unload,' which he did; he also organised some coffee.

He said that both nights were fully booked and we could've sold a lot more tickets. I did wonder if he realised that we were the replacement band. He handed us a copy of the latest *Music Scene*, where Diane's brother had added more publicity about a new band called 'Modern Edge'. We were blown away when we looked at the article and went straight out and bought four copies of the magazine.

Rick was still half asleep from his exploits in shagging for Essex.

'Where'd they dance, then, guv?' said Rick to the manager.

'There's no dancing here,' he replied, 'This is a theatre with 600 seats. I've opened up the sound booth for your sound engineer to get wired up. Coffee will be served in the foyer in a minute. Oh, by the way, I hope you don't mind, I've got the local press coming to see you in a couple of hours' time.'

As he left us, I sat down on one of the seats, so did the other lads. Tony flashed the ash with his Kingsway King Size tipped. Nothing was said until Steve came out with his favourite saying,

'Another fine mess you've got me into, Stanley,' but nobody laughed. I looked at Tony and said,

'Get on the blower to our illustrious leader and ask him why we didn't know anything about this.'

It's the fastest I've seen Tony move since he saw a pound note floating down Barking High Street. To the uninitiated, the reason for the panic was twofold. Number one, we played venues where most of the people came to dance. This meant they weren't looking at you so much, so mistakes could easily be covered up. Number two, in a big theatre like this, the sound coming out of the amps was controlled by a sound engineer in a booth at the back of the theatre. He was the key person. Another worry was that our amps and speakers probably weren't going to be powerful enough for this large auditorium. Now, you can see our predicament. You've got 600 people sitting there looking and listening to every move and sound you make, which is a bit scary. Tony came back after speaking to Mick and said that he'd sent a telegram to Moira's to warn us that a problem was going to arise about needing a sound engineer for this gig.

'Well, I haven't seen any telegram,' I said.

There was a groan from Rick and he pulled out this bit of crumpled paper from his jacket pocket.

'When did you get this, then?' said an annoyed Tony.

'The day we arrived at Moira's.'

'That was ages ago,' I said.

'Trouble with you, Rick,' said Steve, 'Is you think this is just a shagging holiday.'

The pot calling the kettle black came to mind after Steve's comments. The manager called out, 'Coffee's served.'

We went into the foyer and picked up our cups. There was a small ray of sunshine, a pack of Wagon Wheels in their yellow and red wrapping sitting on the tray. After our coffee we walked on to the massive stage while Big Al and some of the theatre stagehands were bringing the gear in. There was one guy in his twenties with a Beatles haircut who seemed to know what he was doing; he was telling the others where they should position the amps and speakers on the stage. All four of us gazed out to the two-tier theatre and the 600 empty seats. In about eight hours they'd be filled with music lovers, expecting us to put on a great show. I shook with fear as I finished the last Wagon Wheel. Tony said,

'Right, we're in the shit and we've got to get on top of this before tonight's performance.'

I stopped the guy with the Beatles haircut who was helping out.

'Thanks for your help, mate.'

'No problem,' he replied.

'What do you do here?' I asked.

'Just help out when bands like yourselves come here.'

'Do you play yourself?'

'Yeah, keyboards, got a group in Sidmouth, called The Vincent Five Blues Band.'

'Have you played here?'

'I wish,' he said, 'This is for the mainline groups like you; we're strictly pubs and local dance halls.'

'Know anything about the sound system here?'

'A little bit, I'm an electrician and keep an eye on all the electrical equipment, which means I get to see all the shows free.'

'You here tonight?'

'Yeah, you bet. Can't wait to hear you. My mate in Taunton saw you a couple of days ago and said you were ace.'

'Do you want to be our sound engineer tonight?'

'What? I don't understand.'

We explained our problem to him; he was lost for words.

'Look,' he said, 'I've been up in the sound booth when groups have come here before, but I've never been hands-on.'

'We need you,' said Steve, 'otherwise we're going to look like a right bunch of amateurs. We'll pay you whatever you want, just help us out.'

'Let's get this straight,' he said, 'you want me to run the sound system for your band tonight?'

'And tomorrow night,' I said. 'By the way, what's your name?'

'Vince.'

'We need you, Vince, what do you say?'

'Yeah. Cool. I'm up for it. But, you've another problem, your speakers and amps don't look powerful enough for this place.'

'That was the next question I was going to ask, can you help?'

'This theatre has its own PA system and I'm sure I can rig something up for you. We'll need to go through the two sets to make sure we're all happy with the sound, but I'll need somebody to help me.'

Tony was the ideal person. The next couple of hours Vince and Tony worked hard. By about two o'clock, we were ready to play the two sets. Before that, two local newspapers turned up and I think we handled ourselves pretty well; it was a new experience for all of us.

I went outside the theatre for some fresh air, and looked up at the posters of us – it was a real turn-on, we were starting to live the dream. When I got back into the foyer, a couple of the girls behind the booking counter asked me for my autograph. One of them was called Carol. This brought back all the emotions of Rod, Carol, Jimmy and the accident. How I wished the three of them were with us now.

We were ready to play the practice session with Vince in the sound booth. The first hour wasn't good, nothing was going right. It only started to sound half decent as we finished the first set. We took a short break and started playing again. The final half hour sounded good and Vince seemed happy with the outcome. We shot back to our digs for a change of clothes and a freshen up. We arrived back to the theatre in plenty of time and were ready to go. The audience were arriving and finding their seats, as we checked everything on stage to ensure that we were ready. The theatre was full and we're on in a few minutes. The four of us shook hands and wished each other good luck. The buzzer went and on we went.

We walked onto the stage to a great reception, picked up our guitars, and were ready to go. This is what it's all about, and it doesn't get any better than this. We were going to start with The Zombies' number 'She's Not There' and then straight into 'Tobacco Road' by The Nashville Teens. Rick gave his chat to the crowd, saying how great it was to be here. I then just happened to focus on the front stalls and saw a wave from the crowd. I looked closer. I couldn't believe it, there was Anita from the hairdressers in Dawlish. I gave her a quick wave back.

We finished the first set which we were all pleased with. Rick's singing was on top form, the air at Burnham-on-Sea must have been doing him some good. We started the second set with 'Suburban Mod'. There's a nice riff to start, and a longish guitar solo part to this number, where I can really express myself. It's a magic feeling as you play your guitar to the maximum, it makes all those hours of practising worthwhile, especially when the audience likes it, as they did on this occasion. It was a nerve-racking two hours playing to 600 people watching your every move, but somehow we survived. All through our performance I was looking at Anita and hopefully she was looking at me. We got a great encore and the crowd kept shouting for more. Vince was a star with the sound system and we made sure he got a loud cheer from the audience when we mentioned his name. After the gig we all went on the beer, met some girls and had a great party around one of their houses. All I can say it was a real Rock 'n' Roll party, full on.

The next day we had massive hangovers so we all agreed to do our own thing, but we all had to make sure we were back at the theatre for two o'clock. We wanted to go over some of the numbers again before the evening's performance, which Vince had agreed to do for us. Vince took to being our sound engineer like a pig to truffles. Steve as usual had pulled a little piece of Devon delight, and was seeing her today. Rick had moved on from Moira and was seeing a girl who he'd met at the party last night, so that was him sorted. Tony was happy going through all our equipment, making sure everything was okay. I'm sure he was still suffering from scrumpy poisoning. It did have a positive effect as he'd pulled a normal bird that didn't scare you. She was one of the booking girls on the front desk at the theatre. She was really nice and kept him supplied with plenty of coffee, and even bought him a fresh Devon clotted cream éclair, now that's love.

Big Al had a deputation from the Exeter Rockers and was being looked after by them. I used the motor and went over to Dawlish to see if I could take Anita out for lunch. It was a long shot but worth a try. I walked into the salon, and she was on her own with no customers. She was well surprised and didn't seem too happy when I walked in.

'What are you doing here, Nick?'

'Well, I wondered if you wanted some lunch.'

'Look, Nick, I'm engaged and I don't think its right to go out with somebody else whose intentions are probably not honourable.'

There wasn't a lot to say as she was spot on.

'Yeah, you're probably right, Anita, it was a worth a try though.'

'I enjoyed your band last night. It's the best band I've heard for a long time,' she said.

'You never told me you were coming.'

'I thought I'd surprise you.'

'Look, I'm going next door for an espresso. If you want to lock up the shop for a few minutes, I'd love to see you, I'll even buy you a coffee and a doughnut.'

I was taking a flyer but I had nothing to lose so I just walked out of the shop to the coffee bar next door. I put a shilling in the jukebox and put on 'Mr Tambourine Man' by the Byrds, 'Help Me Rhonda' by the Beach Boys and 'Concrete and Clay' by Unit 4 Plus 2. I was on my third doughnut when Anita joined me. I got her an espresso but she declined the doughnut. Seeing Robinson's jam dripping off my nose probably put her off. Her boyfriend was called Robin and he worked in the local hardware shop. She'd known him from school and this was the only bloke she'd ever been out with. They were hoping to get married next year. It sounded about as much excitement as a night in watching *Dixon of Dock Green* on the telly with a mug of Bournvita and two digestives. I got the impression that the highlight of the month had been when he took her to the flicks; they'd seen *Breakfast at Tiffany's* last week, exhilarating stuff. I think he preferred a pint with his mates more than taking her out. We had a great hour together, she was a terrific girl. She mentioned it was her day off the next day and she was going shopping in Exeter. She always stayed the night before at her grandparent's house in Exeter.

'Look Anita,' I said, 'I think you're a different class to most of the girls I've met, and I fancy you rotten. I'd love you to come to the gig tonight; I've arranged a seat for you in the front row.' I gave her the ticket. 'Maybe tomorrow, we could spend a few hours together, before I head off for the last part of the tour. What do you say?'

She looked at me for a few seconds, said nothing and walked off. Unfortunately it seemed the charm wasn't working. That was that, then. I forlornly made my way back to Exeter, put the radio on and listened to 'I Got You Babe' by Sonny & Cher. I certainly hadn't got Anita, that was for sure.

The band met up on time and we got stuck into rehearsals. After that we had a couple of hours to spare, so me and Steve decided to try and earn a few bob as we were broke. We thought we'd do some busking in Exeter High Street. So I took my pork pie hat off and placed it on the ground in front of us to collect the money. What a waste of time that was, all we made was half a crown, some French francs, two farthings and two Murray mints. The final indignity was when a poodle cocked its leg up and pissed in my hat.

We went for a Wimpy and arrived back at the theatre in plenty of time. With about an hour to go I popped down into the foyer to get some Woodbines. People were arriving and taking their seats. I noticed a young girl about 12-years-old in a wheelchair being pushed along by a woman in her early thirties, who was probably her mum. The girl's legs were in braces, so life hadn't been too kind to her. They were going out of the theatre, and the young girl was crying. I went over to the mum.

'What's the problem?'

'It's my daughter's birthday today and I've lost the tickets for the show, they won't let us in without them.'

No computer back-up in those days, so no ticket no entry. This wasn't always the case, but as in today's world, there are still jobsworths out there who like their bit of authority. I took them back into the theatre and told them to wait a minute. I went over to the usher and had a word. He was adamant that if they didn't have a ticket they couldn't come in. I didn't have time to argue the toss with him. I asked both the mother and her daughter Claire to wait a minute. I went backstage and had a word with Big Al who was with a girl he'd met that morning. I explained to him about Claire in the wheelchair.

'No problem,' he said, 'they can have our seats and we'll go in the sound booth with Vince. You get back on stage, and I'll go and sort it out, between us we'll give her a great birthday.'

Later on, Big Al cornered the manager and said,

'That was well out of order what one of your staff told that little girl and her mum.'

He was unaware of the incident and went absolutely mad when he heard about it. After the first set he went and found the little girl and her mum, apologised and gave them free tickets for another band that was coming soon. To be fair, when I first met the manager he seemed a really nice guy and this confirmed my thoughts. The jobsworth, I gather, was sent down to the labour exchange with no references!

Just before we started to play I went down to see them in their seats. The little girl and her mother were delighted. As I made my way back to the stage I looked at the empty seat next to Claire and her mum – there was no Anita. We were buzzing, and when we got on stage we received a great reception. The spotlights were on us and we were ready to play. I looked back towards the empty seat again and got a familiar wave – it was Anita, she looked delightful. After that, we had the gig of our life. If you've ever played in a band, you know when one night is special and that was the night. They were rocking in the aisles, we were on top form. At the beginning of the second set, Big Al lifted Claire on to the stage and we got the whole audience to sing happy birthday to her. She loved it and waved to everybody in the audience. The second set went down equally well, and we had a great night. We were blown away with the reception we got; in fact we did two encores. After the gig I met up with Anita, we went for a coffee and just talked. I kissed her goodnight outside her grandparents' house and made arrangements to see her the next day.

The next day I met up with Anita again. We had to leave Exeter late that afternoon, so the boys were picking me up at Exeter railway station later. Anita and I just enjoyed each other's company, she didn't speak about her boyfriend and I never brought the subject up. We went to the La Ronde coffee bar and had our espressos, made with a new Italian La Pavoni espresso machine the owner had just bought. After a great day together, we said our goodbyes and promised we would keep in touch. Her Secret de Venus perfume stayed with me all through the rest of the tour.

We left Exeter for our next port of call, which was Torquay. We arrived at our digs, which were down a dirt track. So far, Mick had been spot on with our overnight stays, but he'd dropped a bollock here. The place looked like Steptoe's yard, thank goodness we were only here for one night. We knocked on the door and a man opened it. He was aged about 35, unshaven and looked filthy. He certainly wasn't in the advert for Colgate Fluoride 'Ring of Confidence' toothpaste, as his teeth were all rotten. Straight away you knew he was injecting, as he had sores all over his arms; we all took an instant dislike to him. It was too late to find somewhere else, so we were there for the night. We were knackered, so we went to bed early, a blessing in disguise as events took over. We'd walked, fed and watered the dog before we got there, so he settled down for the night in the van. He was happy, as he'd had his first bunk up on the tour. Big Al had taken him for a walk in the local park and he'd disappeared for about half an hour. When Big Al finally found him he'd just finished giving this Lassie dog a full seeing to. God knows what the offspring would look like if there was an end product.

We were fast asleep when all hell broke loose. There were yells and ferocious barking coming from the van. We all rushed downstairs including the owner of the B&B. Sampson had two blokes in their mid-twenties pinned up against the van. There was blood everywhere. I've never seen two people look as terrified as those two. Big Al called him off, they sank to the floor, I took a look into the motor and I could see they'd tried to hot-wire the ignition. One of the blokes, who was shaking like a leaf, looked like he was going to have to spend a month with a plastic surgeon. He looked angrily towards the owner of the B&B.

'You didn't tell us … ,' and then he shut up.

'We'd better call an ambulance and the police,' Tony said.

The two blokes and the owner were now in panic mode, and said, 'Don't do that.'

Big Al took over and it wasn't for the faint-hearted. He pulled the two blokes up off the ground and banged their heads together. Their eyes started spinning round like reels in a fruit machine. He looked at the two of them, and pointed towards the owner.

'Was he part of all this?'

The two blokes didn't say anything, so he said to Sampson, 'Bite them again.'

One of them, who was absolutely terrified and had blood spurting from a deep cut on his arm, said,

'No, no, I'll tell you everything.'

The owner had told these two likely lads that we'd be staying there and that there would be a load of musical equipment ripe for nicking. With this info Al went over to the owner and laid him out with one punch. He then went over to the other two blokes, whacked them again and said,

'You tell your mates down the line in Devon and Cornwall that if we find anybody messing about with our van again, they'll be spending a month in hospital after Rin Tin Tin's finished with them, do you get my gist? You two can pay for the damage to the motor, so empty your pockets out, we want some compensation.'

Between them they had £2.3.0d which I took.

'We'll get the rest off your mate later,' Big Al said.

With that, they pulled themselves up and limped away. They kept looking back in case the dog was going to have another go at them. We didn't say anything, but we made a mental note that we wouldn't be upsetting Big Al in a hurry. Joking apart, these two guys were quite badly hurt and it was going through our minds that maybe they'd tell the police what had happened, but they didn't.

The bloke who owned the B&B started to come to after his knock-out blow from Sonny Liston. Big Al got hold of him and frog-marched him back inside the house.

Our bed and breakfast cost us nothing and we got the rest of the money out of him to pay for the damaged ignition, which Tony repaired.

We left and made our way to the hall where we were playing that night. It was a dump and the place was in the middle of a field. Security was useless, so we had to stay with the gear until we played. The bloke who was running the dance looked a sly bastard; he could've been a ringer of the bloke we'd just left at the B&B. He thought he was a flash git and started name-dropping the bands he knew.

'I've had a word with your people,' he said, 'and I'll be putting a cheque in the post.'

We'd just spoken to Mick and he'd said nothing, so we knew he was pulling a fast one. Big Al went back to the van and returned with the dog who was having an off day and kept snarling at everybody. He asked the bloke to repeat himself about the gig money. It all went very quiet as the dog only had eyes for him. He was now having second thoughts about the cheque.

'I'll tell you what,' he said, 'I'll give you the cheque after the gig.'

'No cheques,' Big Al replied. 'You go down to the bank now and get pound notes.'

'I don't know about that.'

He relaxed the lead a bit, and Sampson had another snarl at him.

'I'll get the money right now,' he quickly responded and disappeared.

I popped out to get some grub and came back with sausage sandwiches from a nearby cafe. We gobbled them down even though they were dripping with grease. Then we had a quick soundcheck; everything seemed okay.

Just before we were due to play we all got gut ache and the trots, and there was only one bog in the place. It must have been those sausage sarnies or the fat that was dripping off them. We were really feeling ill and for a while we thought we'd have to cancel. But there were about 200 people coming and we didn't want to let them down, especially as we now had the money in our pocket. It wasn't a good night. Halfway through the first set, Steve, Rick and me had to rush off the stage for a clear out, which left Tony doing a drum solo for about five minutes. Then plugs started to blow on our amps. It was a stop-start performance, but somehow we got through the first set. The bloke who was running the dance came backstage and said he wasn't happy about our amps packing up. I'd never seen Tony lose his rag before, but on this occasion he tore into the bloke and said,

'It isn't our amps, mate, it's your poxy wiring. This place should be condemned. It's a death trap, so piss off.'

We somehow got through the night and thankfully moved on to the next job.

The electrics were always a worry when you were playing, which brings me to a sad story. On the road after a gig you might end up at a transport café on some main road in the dead of night and you often met up with other bands that had been playing. One time we met up with four different bands and had a right laugh. We met up with one band from Cambridge a few times, and even played a gig with them in Bedford. A good few months after that, purely by chance, we saw them again at a petrol station. I noticed that their lead guitarist Shaun wasn't with them. He was a top lad and could he play. We asked where he was. One of the other band members Colin, Shaun's brother, said tearfully that a few weeks back the place where they'd played had dodgy wiring and he'd been electrocuted. We were gutted and didn't know what to say. Colin said they only kept the band together as Shaun would've wanted that. So you can see why we made such a fuss about the electrics when we were playing, because it could be life or death.

We played a few more dance halls in Devon and then it was off to Cornwall.

To give Big Al a rest from driving the van, me and Steve said we'd drive it to the next booking which was in Truro. That was the good news, the bad news was we had to take the dog with us. The other lads left in the Consul and made their way to the gig. They were stopping off at one of Rick's relatives, who had a hotel at St Austell, for cream teas and light ales. The van had been playing up and we'd have to get somebody to have a look at it soon. As we left for Truro with Steve driving, there was black smoke coming out of the exhaust pipe, and it was misfiring big-time.

An hour into the journey and we were looking for a garage to get some petrol. The smoke wasn't letting up and it seemed to be getting worse. It didn't help when we put the radio on and it was playing 'Engine Engine Number Nine' by Roger Miller. We finally pulled into a garage to fill up. This Cornish bloke who was sucking an ice lolly came over to put the petrol in. He was a dry old boy and said,

'I wouldn't bother to put any petrol in this lads, take it over there, that's the place for it,' he said, pointing to a scrapyard.

After filling up with more Redex than petrol, he said,

'The Redex controls smoke emissions, and will help with your problem, until you put a new engine in the van.'

That's all we wanted to hear. Further up the road the dog was getting restless in the back so we stopped for him to have a run, which he did, by chasing poxy rabbits all over this cornfield. It took us ages to get him back in the van and when we did he'd put his feet in a cowpat. The smell was evil and we were heaving.

We finally made it to the outskirts of Truro, and then there was a bang, and the van ground to a halt. Steve looked at me and said,

'There's a church over the road, we'd better go over there and start praying the van hasn't given up the ghost completely.'

We were running behind time as it was, so we had to get something sorted. We lifted up the bonnet to have a look at the engine; I don't know why, because we didn't know anything about motors. In the distance we could see a hearse coming towards us with a number of cars following it. Out of respect we put the bonnet down and took off our pork pie hats, and dipped our heads as the procession made its way in to the church.

We weren't in the AA, we had no money and there was no way we could contact the others. We had to get in touch with Mick, so I took Sampson with me to find a phone box which was two miles away. I scraped together the fourpence for the phone call. Mick wasn't in, so I left a message with his secretary. I tried to ring the dance hall where we were playing, but there was no answer. I trundled back to the van and Steve, and told him we'd run out of options. I would have to go back in an hour to the phone box to see if I could contact anybody. Me and Steve lit up my last two Woodbines. To say we'd had enough was an under-statement, we were supposed to be playing in just under three hours' time. We'd just had our last drag when an empty hearse pulled up in front of us. Steve said with a grin,

'Is it coming for us or the van.'

A lad in his twenties, who was still dressed in his day job clothes, got out of it.

'Can I be of any help?'

'Do I look that bad,' I said.

'Well, I've seen better,' he said with a grin. 'My dad was driving the hearse that passed you an hour back and I was following him in one of the other cars. He was impressed when you two took your hats off in respect. He said that was an unusual thing for the youth of today to do, so much so that he's sent me out to you as I know quite a bit about motors.'

'That's nice of him; we've had our fair share of losing close friends lately, so we respect other people's grief. What's your name?'

'Andy, and another reason I'm here is that I noticed the name of the band on the side of the van. You're playing in town. If I don't sort you out, me and my girl will be disappointed, as we've got tickets to see you tonight.'

Andy had a look under the bonnet, but there was nothing obvious. Time was marching on and we somehow had to get to the gig, then Andy said,

'Right, what we're going to do is load up the hearse with your equipment, and I'll take you to the hall. Then I'll get a mate of mine to tow the van into our yard at work, and I'll have a look at it early tomorrow morning.'

And that's what we did, three blokes, a dog and all our equipment crammed into a hearse. When we entered the car park of the dance hall, the faces of the other three were priceless. The dance hall owner was well pleased to see us as he thought the gig was going pear-shaped since we hadn't shown. One of his stagehands came over to us and said,

'I didn't know 'The Undertakers' were playing here tonight.' (They were an early sixties band out of Liverpool.)

Another one said, 'Who's your singer, Screaming Lord Sutch.' (His party piece was coming out of a coffin on stage before singing.)

The wind-ups continued all night, but it was a great gig, in fact one of the best of the tour. Andy brought the van round to our B&B the next morning.

'The engine is on its last legs,' he said. 'But the problem was a blocked carburettor, so you can continue on with your tour.'

Andy had been a true diamond and we were really grateful to him. As he left, with a big grin on his face, he quipped,

'I hope I don't see you lot again.'

We made our way to the next booking, which was a large caravan park that had its own club house. This was home from home for us as the owners were a family out of Wapping in East London. They made us feel really welcome and had laid on a six-berth mobile home for our overnight stay. We had a meal with the family when we arrived and they let us use their indoor swimming pool. Then it was back to business for the dance tonight. The place seemed full of Geordies and a few of the birds came over to see us while we were setting up; we couldn't understand what they were saying. Tony and Rick got off the mark quickly with two girls from Newcastle, in fact it was so quick they disappeared with them within two minutes. That left me and Steve to set up the show and get everything in order for the night, which we weren't happy about. Even Big Al had done a runner for the afternoon; he'd met another dog lover and had gone back to her kennel! We finally finished, and didn't even have time to go back to the mobile to put on a clean tee-shirt. We were half an hour away from when the gig was due to start, and there was no sign of Tony and Rick. The hall was packed with holidaymakers and they were waiting for us to play. Big Al then sauntered in looking very happy with himself after his afternoon at Crufts.

'Have you seen the other two on your travels?' I asked.

'Yeah, I saw them go into a caravan a while back.'

He told us where it was, so me and Steve rushed round there. It wasn't much of a caravan, it looked a heap, it's a wonder you could get four people in it. I gave the door a kick and shouted out to the two of them. At either end of the caravan two little windows opened, with the grinning faces of Tony and Rick. I was starting to lose it and let them have both barrels.

'We're on in a few minutes, you two jokers,' I said.

'Is it that time already?' said Rick, who wasn't taking it seriously.

Steve then pulled the door open, went inside and in between the screams from the two naked girls, hauled Rick and Tony out, who were in a state of undress, and marched them back to the hall. We just about started on time. It was going well until the Geordies wanted us to play every Animals number they'd ever done. (The group were out of Newcastle.) We only knew 'The House of the Rising Sun', so they weren't happy with that.

In spite of everything it was a good night. We'd just finished the last number, when Tony and Rick left the stage and made off with these two girls again. Steve looked at me and said,

'Right, those two are going to have some.'

Big Al had felt guilty about leaving us this afternoon, so said he'd put everything away in the van himself. He did have some help, as two young sons of the owner came over to give him a hand. This was great, as me and Steve were going to get our own back on the other two. We crept up on the girl's caravan and waited until the lights went out. We gave it a few minutes; we knew that the two of them were at either end of the caravan with their Geordie birds. We went to one end of the caravan and gently rocked it a few times. This was Tony's end and he shouted out to Rick,

'Christ, Rick, calm it down, you're making me seasick with all this rocking.'

We then went to Rick's end and did the same thing there, so Rick shouts out to Tony,

'Can't you do it a bit slower, it's like a bleedin' earthquake at my end.'

Me and Steve are in tears. How we held it together I don't know. We did it a couple more times, and in the end Tony, Rick and the two girls are all shouting and arguing with each other to stop rocking the caravan, as it's putting them off their stroke. We had one final trick up our sleeve. We had taken a couple of fire extinguishers out of the hall. We stopped a couple of people and told them what we were up to. They were up for it, and they shouted out 'Fire, Fire' a couple of times outside the girl's caravan. It didn't take long before Tony and Rick shot out of the door with nothing on, and for their troubles they got well drenched. After that there was no more disappearing from those two.

The next gig was at Newquay, not a bad one, until a bunch of Mods from Manchester and another bunch from Liverpool decided to have a punch-up on the dance floor. They were all staying at a nearby holiday camp. We'd just finished a Dave Clark Five number, 'Glad All Over', which was the starting point for the first chair to go through a window. Sampson was brought on stage to protect us and the gear, until the police arrived. Then four Mods saw Rocker Big Al, and thought they'd give him a seeing to, but they didn't see his mate. As they attempted to have a pot at him, the dog came out of the shadows and took an almighty lump out of one of the Mod's arses. His mohair suit was now in rags, he screamed the place down and ran off. Only two policemen turned up and they couldn't control them; one of the Mods punched one of them to the ground. We all ran over to their rescue and surrounded the two coppers until others arrived. Big Al let the dog run loose and he sorted out the 20-plus Mods all on his own. As soon as they saw him, they ran in all directions and by the time police reinforcements arrived they'd all disappeared. The gig was cancelled, of course, and we had an early bath as they say, but got paid for it. The police were very grateful and thanked us all. They wanted Big Al's details to put in their report, but he gave them a false name and address. We didn't ask why, but he must have had his reasons.

Now Rick could sleep through a storm. One of the digs we stayed at in Cornwall was right by the beach. Early one morning the rest of us lifted up his bed while he was still fast asleep, took it over to the beach and left it there. The four of us went back for our breakfast; from the window we could see Rick. The tide was coming in and he was still out like a light. The water was almost on top of him when he awoke. He'd had a good few beers the night before, and was in a dream when he woke up. We had a right giggle when he attempted to get out of bed and fell straight into the sea. He was splashing about like a drowned rat and wasn't a happy little soldier. We went over to the beach to take the piss out of him. Sampson, seeing Rick splashing about, bounded towards him, jumping on top of him and pushing him back into the sea. The joke backfired on us, as we had to pay the landlady for a new Z-bed.

Later on in the tour we had a day off and I went by train to see Anita while the others did their own thing. Anita met me at Exeter station, looking really nice. She greeted me like she really wanted to see me, we went to a milk bar and had two lime milk shakes. She told me she'd broken off her engagement. Before I could say anything, she said that after meeting me, she'd realised that only ever having the one boy friend wasn't for her. There was a lot more to life and she was too young to settle down. We knew there was no way that our relationship would work long-term so we enjoyed the time we had together. She was a terrific girl and maybe, who knows, something might happen in the future for us. We had a great day but it was back on the train to Cornwall for me.

Tony and Rick had met these two Rocker girls and spent all day with them at one of the girl's houses, and they weren't playing snakes and ladders. They were full of it when they got back to our B&B. The next night we played the gig and Tony and Rick played the pop stars card and invited the girls to the dance. As we were playing, the girls danced in front of them all night. To be fair, we've all done it. At the end of the night we were packing the gear into the van while Big Al took Sampson for a walk. Suddenly about six Rockers in their twenties surrounded us, and from the look of their faces they weren't happy. Two of them were the boyfriends of Tony and Rick's conquests the day before. They made it quite clear that we were going to get a good hiding. They came at us, we weren't ready, and they started to pile into us. We were taking a bit of a pasting until Tony picked up one of his cymbals and smacked one of the guys over the head with it. The sound of the cymbal making contact with the bloke's head, and then his loud scream had an immediate effect. Big Al heard it and raced back to the van with Sampson. As soon as our attackers saw the dog they were off on their motorbikes as fast as Geoff Duke.

We woke up the next morning with lumps and bruises, well and truly pissed off, until Tony phoned Mick. He came back and said,

'Some great news. A guy from a record company came to see us play at Exeter, they want us to go into their studio and record a couple of numbers. That's not all, one of the big national dance hall promoters also wants to hear us play, and maybe sign us up.'

We were overwhelmed with the news and couldn't wait to finish our last gig that night in Penzance. The other thing that was overwhelmed was the Ford Consul; the engine blew up.

'It would help if you put some Duckham's oil in it,' I said to Rick, who was in charge of the motors. We took it to a scrapyard and got a few quid for it which paid for the petrol home.

Before the last gig in Penzance we had a day off; we met some local girls and took them down to the beach. They took the rise out of us because our faces and bodies were as white as snow. It was the height of summer and we looked out of place on the beach. One of the girls said,

'Leave it to me, I'll get you some instant tan.'

She left and came back with a large plastic bottle of the stuff. We thought it was a good idea to get an instant tan, as the folks back home would see that we'd had a good time, and we'd look nice and healthy. This girl slapped it on our faces. One of the other girls said she was applying far too much of the stuff and wasn't spreading it evenly enough. We didn't care, as her soft slim hands with painted fingernails were very therapeutic. This was another girl who had magic in her hands; it was a pity we were going home tonight. Tomorrow, she said, we'd all wake up as brown as berries.

After the last show that night we all got in the van to travel home through the night. We put the radio on and 'One Way Love' by Cliff Bennett & The Rebel Rousers came on. We were reflecting on the tour which we all felt had been great. We'd made no money because we'd spent it all enjoying ourselves, but we'd had a great time, and with the promise of maybe a record contract, and working for a big dance hall organisation, life was looking sweet.

Imagine this; you've a full load of equipment, five blokes who could all do with a Camay bath, including their clothes and a dog as big as a house all crammed into a van. All we had to smoke was a special Nosegay roll-up. We had a few cans of Ind Coope Long Life beer, and some individual Lyons fruit pies. We shared the driving and by the time we'd got to Wiltshire they were all fast asleep except for me. I was at the wheel, but getting a bit kippy, so I tried to park the van up somewhere.

æ æ æ

The entire band knows I'm as blind as a bat, but I won't wear glasses because I'm vain, and I reckon the birds don't fancy blokes with glasses. I finally park the van up and get my head down. The next morning we're all woken up by the sound of traffic around us, but take no notice, as we're all dying for a jimmy. It's still dark as we all get out of the van half asleep to have one. There we are, five blokes in a line and a dog. Then somebody toots their horn, we all look up and there's a coach load of old girls, which has come to a standstill on the roundabout, and they're all looking at us and laughing.

'Who parked here last night?' said Steve, 'It's only on a bloody roundabout on a main road.'

'It was dark,' I said. (I remember another time we were coming back from a gig in Northampton and had parked in a field about three in the morning for some shut-eye. We were awoken by the van being violently rocked from side to side.

We looked out and there was this bleedin' great bull giving the van a Glasgow kiss.)

A couple of miles up the road, it's just starting to get light, and we stop at a transport café for breakfast. We're still half asleep as we make our way into the crowded café. Inside there are some lorry drivers having their breakfasts, and some of them are pointing at us and taking the piss. We ain't happy and go over to the smallest one.

'What's the joke mate?' Rick asks.

'Don't you know?'

'I wouldn't ask if I knew,' replied Rick, who's now got the right cob on.

'Look in the mirror.'

'What?' said Rick.

A lady and her family were sitting at the same table as the driver. She takes a make-up mirror out of her bag and puts it in front of Rick's face and then ours. Our faces are all blotchy and bright orange. Everyone in the café falls about laughing, including us. The orange look stayed with us for a couple of weeks.

ào ào ào

We got home later that day. We had a week off and I spent most of it in bed, I was all in. We had to make some more money, so we went back on the road, and hopefully we'd make a record and sign up with this dance hall promoter. We'd now made it, we thought, and we're going to be the next Beatles, and star on *Ready Steady Go*. I was already planning what colour I was going to have on my new E-type Jag.

As we know, life's not like that. Things come back and haunt you, when you get a bit cocky and you're not expecting it, and that's what happened to us. When I came back off tour I thought, stupidly, I could pick up with the lovely Diane. Wrong, she'd moved on and that didn't include me. We were still good friends but nothing else. After that, it all went downhill; the so-called record company deal came to nothing. We had to do an audition for this company who owned a lot of dance halls in the UK, and were looking for bands to play these venues. Their offices were in Tottenham Court Road, in London's West End.

এ এ এ

First of all, we can't get the poxy van to start, so that put us back an hour. Then the traffic around this area is horrendous. One of the back streets behind the company's building has road works, so we can't get down there. We're now running late, so Tony does a sharp left and puts the van outside the front entrance. Steve rushes into the building to tell them we're here. He comes back and tells us we're to set up in the large reception area. So we work our nuts off, unload the gear and set up in record time. We can't move the van because we're late, so it has to stay there. It's now causing traffic congestion on the Tottenham Court Road. The powers that be in the company come out of their offices to listen to us. We go straight into our own number, 'Suburban Mod', followed by a couple of covers. Then one of my strings breaks, so I have to mess about with that. Then a whole army of school kids on a day out to London are walking past the building and spot us playing in the reception area. They like what they hear, so stop and put their noses up against the window. Some of them even come into where we're playing. Now this has caught the attention of other people walking by and they, too, stop to watch and listen. So there's a big crowd inside and outside the building, and now the police are involved as the van's holding up all the traffic, and the pavement is completely blocked. We've lost it and we're starting to play crap. Two coppers, who look well past their sell-by date, barge through the crowd and into the reception area where we're playing. You can see the coppers are not interested in our type of music or us; they look like Max Bygraves and Guy Mitchell fans. They are hell-bent on cocking it up for us, and they do.

'Stop playing and move the van now or you'll be arrested for breach of the peace and unauthorised parking.'

Of course, we stop playing which upsets the kids who kick off and start having a go at the two coppers. It's complete and utter mayhem. More police are called; the teachers are trying desperately to round the kids up and we're in the middle of it all. The classy reception area is ruined, a couple of our amps and a speaker get slightly damaged, and that's the end of that. The next booking at a church youth club in Epsom is rather tame by comparison.

❧ ❧ ❧

Mick's mum died, which was sad, but it was even sadder for us, as she'd left him loads of money and he was now pulling out of the music business and moving to live in Spain. So by the end of 1965 our band had no manager, not many gigs booked and no money. In fact it looked like the band was coming to an end.

1966

The stolen Football World Cup trophy is found in South
   London by a mongrel dog called Pickles.
The UK has its first push-button phone.
The Breathaliser test arrives for UK motorists.
The first British credit card is introduced by Barclaycard.
Gangster Ronnie Kray shoots George Cornell in the Blind
   Beggar pub in East London.
The science fiction programme Star Trek has its first episode on
   television – 'The Man Trap'.
The Aberfan disaster occurs in South Wales – 116 children and
   28 adults are buried alive.
Freddie Laker launches his Laker Airways.
Comedian Arthur Haynes dies.
George Harrison marries Pattie Boyd.
Double agent George Blake escapes from Wormwood Scrubs.
The last episode of Ready Steady Go is broadcast, hosted by
   Cathy McGowan.
The Rolling Stones have a Number One hit with 'Paint It Black'.
The Soviet Luna 9 spaceship lands on the moon.
'We're more popular than Jesus, now,' says John Lennon.
Ring-pulls are introduced on soft drinks cans in the UK.
England win the football World Cup, beating Germany 4-2.
The Hawker Harrier is the world's first vertical take-off plane.
Twiggy is nominated Face of the Year by The Daily Express.
Buster Keaton, star of the silent screen, dies.
Watney's increases beer prices by a penny a pint to 1/8d.
John Ridgway and Chay Blyth row across the Atlantic.
Walt Disney passes away.

♪ 18 ♪

It's Not Looking Too Good

The first week in January, we all met up round my house to discuss where the group was going or, more to the point, wasn't going. Big Al had gone back to whatever he did before following the tour to the west country. We kept in close contact with him, as he'd been a great mate. There was also some sad news, with the death of Denny, who played drums for us at the Burnham-on-Sea gig. He'd died of a drugs overdose.

I must have had some influence with Anita from Dawlish. After meeting me, as mentioned, she felt there was more to life than what she had, so she moved to Reading to stay with her sister. She was now working as a hairdresser in the town. We're still close in a funny sort of way and have met up a couple of times. The chemistry's still there and ongoing.

We had bookings for about three months, which Mick had put in place before he departed to a sunnier climate. Tony had got in touch with the places we were playing at and sorted the finance out. This way we knew we had money coming in.

But it was crunch time. Should we disband the group, find someone else to represent us and carry on, or go part-time and find a job? We all wanted to continue with the group, as we all felt we had a great sound. It's in times like this that you pull together. Except for the money we were all having a great crack. There were plenty of girls and plenty of laughs to be had and we were enjoying the music that we were playing. We all agreed the priority was to find an agent and get some more bookings in place. In the meantime the existing gigs had to be played and there were some good, bad, ugly and some unusual ones. Let's start with the latter.

We had a gig in Southend at a dance hall. We went there early as Southend is full of local beauties. We thought we'd have a wander along the sands, or rather mud, to see if any of them were about. The miniskirt was still playing havoc with our hormones and we couldn't get enough of it. We went to the dance hall just after lunch. They had good security there and you could lock your gear away, so we thought we'd drop it off early and have a gander around the lust pots of Southend. When we got to the hall there were loads of noisy brats, a right bunch of scallywags. They were having some sort of party, as there were balloons and food all over the place. We all looked at each other and thought, let's get out of here quick. We saw the caretaker and started to unload our van. As we were doing so, a vicar came out of the hall and looked at our musical gear.

'Are you a band?' he asked.

'You're spot on, vic,' replied Rick, 'we're playing here tonight.'

We didn't see it coming, did we? All we were thinking of was being on Southend Pier and ogling all the girls going by.

'Look, lads,' said the vicar, 'I know it's a bit of a cheek, but could you spare an hour of your time?'

'What's that for then, vic?' asked Rick.

'We've over 150 under-privileged children who've come down from London. London taxi drivers bring them down every Easter for a day out. In some cases they've never ever seen the seaside before or been taken out anywhere, so we try and give them a good time on their day here.'

'I'm not sure what you mean,' said Rick.

'Well, could I ask you to play to them for an hour, before they go back to their various Barnado's homes?'

Rick stood there and looked like he was chewing a wasp. The vicar could see from our faces that it hadn't hit the right note. Then a right looking little urchin of about 11, wearing a party hat, came out of the hall and looked at the guitar I'm holding.

'Are you coming to play for us, mister? I like The Beatles.'

He could see from our faces we didn't want to, and we blanked him.

In a strong cockney accent he looked at us and said,

'I bet you lot are crap anyway.'

He grinned, then poked his tongue out, gave us the 'v' sign and disappeared back into the hall. We fell for it, didn't we, and played to them for an hour. They were jiving and twisting and really enjoying themselves. Rick started a conga and took them around the hall, outside and back again. They were having a ball and, to be fair, so were we. I found out from one of the taxi drivers that most of the kids had no parents and this was the highlight of their year. We finished the hour and it was time for them to go back to London. The little urchin who we met first came over to us and said,

'I was right, then, you lot *are* a load of rubbish. I've heard better sounds coming from the Salvation Army.'

We chased him back into the hall to try and get hold of him, but he was too quick for us and disappeared out of sight.

The evening gig didn't go down so well either, as there was a punch-up on the dance floor, but somehow we got through the evening without getting involved. Then we got knocked for the gig money by the promoter. We also ran out of petrol in the middle of nowhere and we had no money. Rick's dad had to come out with a gallon of petrol, and he wasn't happy.

We played another local dance hall every other week. This one had only opened a few months previously, a right flea-pit, and it wasn't our favourite place to play. I don't know how people could afford to go there, as they charged top whack to get in. We saw Alec and a few of our friends outside the dance hall when we next played there, and asked that very question. Alec was the guy whose parties we used to go to, which had now ceased. This was due to him leaving a Player's Weight cigarette burning on his mother's downstairs table while he was having a hands-of-the-desert moment upstairs. Unfortunately, while he was getting his wicked way, the house caught alight. When his parents came back, they weren't impressed with the three fire engines sitting outside their house, so 'The Half a Dozen Club', which we were founder members of, was no longer.

Back to the flea-pit, I'm saying to Alec, 'How'd you afford to keep coming here?'

'You want to know how we can afford it?' They all started to laugh.

'It's easy,' he said. 'When you want to go to the toilet, you have to go outside the hall. As you go out, they stamp a number on your arm in indelible ink, so they know you've already paid when you come back in.'

'You've lost me,' I said.

Alec and the rest of them started laughing again. They then pull their shirts and jumpers up, and they've got these numbers stamped on their arms. There was a 36, 41, 131 and so on.

'But the dance hall isn't open yet, so how can you have these stamped on your arms already?' I said.

'Easy,' Alec replied. 'When we first started coming here a few weeks ago, we paid first time around,' then he looked at one of the lads, called Joe.

'Joe works for a chemical company. He came up with a solution that if you put a dab of it on the number on your arm, you can't wash it off, unless you scrub it hard. So its freeman's every time we go in. You have to give it a bit of time for the hall to fill up before you go in, otherwise it looks a bit dodgy.'

It was a great scam but it didn't help us, as the dance hall went tits up and out of business a couple of weeks later. I wonder why. This meant of course we lost two bookings a month, so they had to be replaced.

I still hadn't thanked Pete for writing the articles about the band in *Music Scene*, which I felt guilty about. The next day I phoned Diane to get her brother's phone number. She gave me the number and I tried the old chat-up line as I still fancied her. There was hope of a date as she wasn't sold on her new bloke, and she told me to keep in touch. Now I was on the plot I'd be ringing her up every week until she said yes.

The gigs we were doing were all over the place, and to be honest most of them were dross. You went from a spit-and-sawdust pub in the dock area of London, playing to a load of piss heads, and then it would be some run-down church hall in deepest Lincolnshire. We once had to go to a coffin dodger's place in Clacton, and play to an over-seventies club. All they wanted was bleedin' Vera Lynn, Gracie Fields, Russ Conway and Glen Miller. The ultimate was at a borstal playing to a load of tearaways. You couldn't even go for a piss in case they nicked the gear.

We were sinking fast, and the dream of being a big player in the pop industry was waning by the day. Mick had left us a load of jobs that nobody else wanted. We were hardly getting any money, and the van was due for the scrappers. Our love lives were on melt down, as by the time we put the gear back onto the van after the gig, it was well past midnight and we had to drive home or on to the next job. There were no bed and breakfast stays anymore, the van was where we lived, slept and ate. We played three towns in Derbyshire on the trot, and all we had to eat for the first two days was a tanner's worth of stale cakes from a bakers in Burton-on-Trent. Our luck changed on the third and final day when we met some girl students and went back to their house. We went through their larder like wild animals and stuffed ourselves with their grub. Mind you, we did leave enough room for dessert, which took all night to sample.

We were now starting to get arsy with each other and the sparkle we had at the beginning of the year had nearly gone. It was crunch time and we had only 20 gigs left. There were no more in the pipeline and none of us had the energy or the inclination to go and find more work. We were all getting into debt and were borrowing money from our parents, who could ill afford it. This had to stop and we'd near enough decided to jack it in. From the heady days of playing in front of 600 at a theatre in Exeter, we were now playing to just a handful of people in smoke-filled dives.

On a day off I met up with Anita who looked great. She had this Newsboy cap on and a pair of brown Hush Puppies, which I wasn't quite sure about. She was really enjoying her new life in Reading and was doing well for herself. In fact, in the next few weeks she was getting her own flat. The slightly shy Devon girl was now confident and even lovelier. She'd immediately picked up that I wasn't the same bloke she'd met last year, who was full of cheek. I told her the sorry state of the group and that we were probably going to call it a day.

'That's not like you,' she said, 'I thought you Essex boys were made of stronger stuff than that.'

Now where've I heard that before? In fact she had a right pop at me for giving up so easily and even bollocked me for the state of my unkempt hair. After coffee and a knickerbocker glory at the Tropicana coffee bar, where as usual half of it went down my jumper, we went back to her sister's place where she gave me a haircut.

'But I'm not washing it,' she said with a grin. 'That's better. All you need now is a bath.'

I looked at her and before I could say anything she said,

'No, I'm not giving you one of those either.'

We said our goodbyes and she made me promise that I'd keep going with the band. For a minute I nearly suggested us living together. I'd pack up the group and move up here to be with her and get a job. I was just about to go when she said, 'I nearly forgot,' and handed me a film.

'What's this? A bluee?'

'One track mind,' she said. 'No, it was taken by a friend of mine, when you played the second night at Exeter. I went back home a few weeks ago and he'd left it round my mum's house for me. He's a photographer and saw you play the first night and thought you were really good. The theatre manager is a good friend of his and allowed him back the next night to film you performing. This is a copy; he's kept the original as he reckons you'll be famous someday.'

'Have you seen it?'

'You must be joking? I can't afford a projector to play that. Show it to the other lads in the band, it just might change your mind about packing it up.'

We said our goodbyes again, which lasted about another half an hour and it was back to Essex and the next night's gig.

This gig was not dross. Mick had excelled himself. Perhaps he'd felt sorry for us and had given us a bit of cream, which made a change. We deserved it, as the one before this we'd played to an OAP club in Frinton-on-Sea. This is a town in Essex where they like you to be over 80-years-of age before they let you move there. They thought they'd booked a magician; excuse the joke, we disappeared a bit quick from there. There was one good thing, the cocoa and those Jacob's lemon puffs were really nice!

This great gig gave us back a bit of our pride. We were playing for a well-known airline. They were having a reception for all the new air hostesses who'd just passed out and were now qualified. It was held at one of the top hotels near London Airport. With all the family members, airline staff and the hangers-on, there was a lot of people there. Once all the presentations were given, it was party time. We started off with 'Mirror Mirror' by Pinkerton's Assorted Colours, then on to 'Keep on Runnin' by Spencer Davis Group and then straight into 'Get off of My Cloud' by The Rolling Stones, which we thought was quite apt.

All four of us had been on rations re the sexual side of our relationships lately, so we were looking for a change of luck. Looking at all the girls there, we felt that this could be the night. At the finish of the first set, a few girls came over to see us. Me and Steve had our eyes on two of the newly qualified air hostesses in their brand new uniforms. They were very chatty and we made arrangements to meet them afterwards. We couldn't wait to finish the second set. We started off with 'Wild Thing' by The Troggs, then on to 'Hold Tight' by Dave Dee, Dozy, Beaky, Mick & Titch, and then on to our own material which went down well. The last number we played was a nice slow one, 'A Groovy Kind of Love' by The Mindbenders, which we dedicated to the two girls we'd just met. Steve's girl was Susie and mine was Pauline. I knew she was for me, especially her perfume, White Fire, it was overwhelming, and I was in love – again.

After the gig, we had a drink at the bar with the girls and it was apparent that the four of us had some energy to burn. Both the girls had rooms booked in the hotel, and later me and Steve spent the night with them. I had a nice gentle take-off with Pauline, and then halfway through the journey had a couple of drinks off the trolley. When it was time to come into land, it was soft and safe. Steve had a great take-off with Susie and then quite a bit of turbulence on the flight. On coming into land, it was very bumpy and they nearly came off the runway.

While having breakfast in Pauline's room the next morning she said,

'You'll have to go soon, I'm flying to New York later.'

'That's all right,' I replied, 'I'm off to Sidcup in a van for a gig.'

Tony had struck lucky with a girl from Customs and Excise, who stamped his card all night. Rick, being Rick, had double bubble with two girls, who were from the admin department of the company; they'd organised the event for the airline. They'd booked the rooms for everybody, and also booked themselves a nice suite, so tricky Ricky had come out on top as usual, sweet as a nut.

♪ 19 ♪

Things are Looking Better – or are They?

We played the gig at Sidcup which was in a seedy club. There were plenty of drugs on show, mostly amphetamines, like Dexedrine. The place got raided by the police while we were playing, and we were told to pack up and leave; that was another gig we didn't get paid for. We'd somehow got a few more bookings but we were still draining money and it had to stop. The following Sunday we weren't playing, and were all going round Rick's to have a chat with his dad, who, as I said before, had a large haulage business, and was a shrewd operator. I still hadn't rung Diane's brother Pete, to thank him for the article, which I felt a bit guilty about. So on the Saturday before, I gave Pete a bell. What a nice guy he was. He asked me about the band and, of course, I told him we were thinking of packing it in. I told him about going around Rick's and he asked if he could come along, as he had a couple of ideas. He only lived in Harold Wood so Brentwood was just up the road to him.

Sunday morning we all went to see Rick's dad, Mr. Brady. It was a nice house with a big driveway. It was a pity that oil was gushing out of the sump of our van all over his nice driveway. Pete was introduced to everybody, a snappy dresser in his late twenties. Mr. Brady was going to give us his opinion of our problems. Rick's dad was as modern as you could get at the ripe old age of 40; he did seem to understand modern youth, but thought hair down to your shoulders was a bit nancy boy. He was a man who, I would think, wouldn't suffer fools gladly and he had an air about him. I'd brought the film along, as Mr. Brady had a top of the range film projector. We were expecting some joke production and we were ready to take the rise out of ourselves. Mr. B, as we now called him, set the film in motion. We were well taken aback at the quality and the sound of it. It was a real professional production and we just watched and listened to ourselves. We always felt that this was the best we'd ever played. After about 20 minutes we stopped the film. Pete, said,

'I've never heard you play before and I did the short article on the hoof, as a favour to my sister and your former manager, but I have to say, you lot have got something special going for you and you can't pack it in now. Your own number, 'Suburban Mod', is a winner. It needs to be polished up a bit, but it sounds great.'

'Appreciate your kind comments, Pete,' Tony said, 'But we ain't got a pot to piss in. We've no manager, no agent, no money, we're all in debt, the van's due for the scrapyard, and we've only got about a dozen bookings left.'

'Apart from that,' said Steve, 'we're in pretty good shape.'

We all agreed that the sound was pretty cool and we were tight as a band. It made us think that we had something to work on, but investment was the priority if we were going to be able to keep going. Mrs. B brought in a tray of goodies to eat and some of that real Maxwell House coffee, not the Camp stuff my mum made. Mr. B asked Pete to step outside to have a chat, while we had another look at the film. That's when the mickey-taking started. Steve was giving it the business on his bass guitar on this particular song, and he was showing off. When you looked closely, he hadn't plugged his guitar into the amp, so there was no sound coming out. Mind you, Steve was one of the best bass players around.

The banter went on for a good half an hour until Mr. B and Pete came back. Mr. B quickly took charge and said to us,

'Stop the cackle and listen up as I've plenty to say. Right, I might not know much about your modern music, but Pete does, he thinks you've got what it takes, and I must admit you sound pretty good. Pete knows quite a lot of people in the music industry and he's going to try to find you a reliable agent who won't rip you off. He'll also advise me musically and, of course, you, in where we should be going. Secondly, if you agree, I'll become your manager and look after your affairs. I'll bank roll you for six months, then we'll re-examine it. As my son's with you, you've got no problem about being fitted up by me. If you make it and are successful we'll split the money five ways. That means you four and me. Pete is going to be on a retainer from me to look after your musical interests. You all looked like a bag of Murphy's spuds on that film, so you're going to be fitted out with some new clobber. I've got a Ford Transit Van for all of your equipment. Pete reckons that song of yours, 'Suburban Mod', needs re-arranging, so he's going to contact someone with a recording studio. He'll get you in there, cut a demo disc and canvass the record companies. Any questions?'

There were none.

'One of my lorry driver's mates, Gordon, will act as your roadie for the time being.'

We got kitted out with our new mohair suits and Brutus button-down shirts, courtesy of John Collier. We also got ourselves a short lightweight Harrington jacket which had a check patterned lining and some Chelsea boots with Cuban heels. We now looked like an original Mod band and were moving forward again. The Transit had the band's name plastered all over it. Pete did the business and found us an agent who came to see us play in London. He liked what he heard and started fixing us up with some dates. We were getting about £5 each a gig. Unfortunately me and Steve couldn't play football anymore because of our commitments and when England were beating West Germany in the World Cup final we were on our way to Grantham, listening to it on the radio. The England team had some great players like Alan Ball, Bobby Charlton, Gordon Banks, Nobby Stiles and Bobby Moore. When Geoff Hurst scored the fourth goal we nearly crashed the van.

I was still in close contact with Anita and met up with her a number of times. When we had a booking in Reading she came and watched us play. She'd blossomed into a great girl and was now working as a hairdresser in the West End of London on bundles of money. I still had a bit of cheek left in me and asked her if she'd give the boys in the band a haircut before we played the gig in Reading. She did.

♪ 20 ♪

Rhodes – Where's That?

We were playing from Dunstable to Shrewsbury, Doncaster
to Birmingham and Manchester to Newcastle; we even played
Dundee in Scotland. The money was good and we were
having a ball. Some of the parties were wild, and the drink
flowed. We were living the dream of wine, women, song and
Woodbines. Then out of the blue we had a real taster. The
two girls that Rick had shared his passions with at the airline
party got in touch with him. They asked if the band would
like to play for a party of airline people for two nights. We'd
be staying for three days in a five-star hotel in Rhodes in four
weeks' time. The hotel would have all the musical equipment
available as they had a resident band. All we had to do was
bring our guitars. Our expenses would be taken care of and
the money on offer was equivalent to about two weeks' work
for us. Rick immediately said yes; remembering the night he
spent with them before, he'd have done it for nothing. The
bonus for him was that they were coming too. We got a letter
the next day confirming all the details. We were playing locally
at a college that night. After we'd set up on stage we had an
hour to spare. Rick pulled the letter out of his pocket. We
all lit up some American Lucky Strikes. After a good cough,
Rick explained about the call and we read the letter. First of
all, nobody knew where Rhodes was.

'Is it one of the Channel Islands?' said Steve.

'No, near the Isle of Man,' said Tony.

'Somewhere near Spain,' said Rick.

'America,' I said, because I'd heard of Rhode Island in the USA.

What a load of jodrells, we hadn't got a clue. The girl who was looking after us looked quite bright, so we asked her.

'Oh,' she said, 'That's a Greek island, I know all about it. It's the largest island in the archipelago called Dodecanese, and is the capital of that group of Greek islands. The capital of Rhodes lies outside but within the walls of a very well preserved Venetian castle … '

'That's really good, luv, I'm well impressed,' I said. Talk about feeling a thicko.

There were two problems; none of us had ever been abroad before, except to the Isle of Wight, so we'd got no passports. Secondly the dates clashed with two gigs in Cleethorpes. No disrespect to Cleethorpes, but it ain't Rhodes, so it was no contest, but Rick's dad wasn't going to be happy if we broke an agreement with the agent. So far, we'd done everything we'd been asked to do, but the sun, girls and the thought of playing in Rhodes was a bigger attraction than Cleethorpes. At the time Rick's dad seemed to have more pressing things on his mind, so we felt we could manipulate him. To be fair, the airline and the two girls helped us get our passports quickly.

In between we'd been to the studio to record a couple of numbers, which sounded half decent. Pete had arranged this for us, but like Rick's dad, he seemed to have other things on his mind. Anyway, we were off to sunny Greece, it was about time we had a holiday. We phoned the agent up a few days before the gigs in Cleethorpes and said Rick had lost his voice. He wasn't happy, but he'd get over it. We bunged Gordon the roadie a few quid and told him to make himself scarce for a few days; he was about our age and not a bad lad.

We arrived at London Airport and were ready for some fun. Me and Steve carried our guitars with us, all four of us looking and acting like budding pop stars, with our tonic suits, pork pie hats and dark shades. Sad, ain't it? Tony had a bag with Comet in bold embossed letters on the side, which didn't make me feel too safe. Do you remember your first flight? This was ours and we were crapping ourselves. As the plane took off, we all looked at each other and said our goodbyes. Once we were up in the air everything seemed fine and we felt a bit happier. After a couple of brandies we were seasoned travellers and enjoying the experience, especially the air hostesses.

The other people that were travelling were on a jolly-up. They were mostly travel agents who'd reached the airline's sales targets and had been rewarded with this short trip. We flew into Athens for the connecting flight to Rhodes. The sight of the blue sea as we landed was stunning, a bit different from the sea at Clacton. As we got off the plane, the heat hit you, a new experience for us. The next plane to Rhodes was a propeller job. As we boarded this old prop plane none of us felt too safe. The pilot walked through from the back of the plane to the cockpit, as he couldn't get the front entry door open. We christened him Pedro the Pilot, as he had his airline hat sitting on the side of his head, and was smoking a stinky fag. Somehow we took off; it felt like we were skimming the waves and we didn't seem to be very high up. Thankfully we arrived safely and the four of us clapped as we landed, much to the amusement of the other passengers.

We were taken by coach to the Rhodes Sea Hotel, which looked magnificent. As we were playing in three hours we dropped our cases into our rooms, all with balconies. We went straight to where we would be playing to have a look at the equipment the hotel had provided. It was a nightclub and the in-house sound equipment was top dollar. A couple of the resident band members were on hand to show us the ropes. We had no complaints; we had a quick soundcheck and everything was in order. The lead guitarist of the hotel band let me use his new wah-wah pedal which alters the tone of a guitar; it brought a new dimension to my playing. It was the first time I'd used one, and it was definitely on my wish list. I really gave it a bit of pedal over the next two nights.

As the four of us were getting everything ready on stage, a few girls popped over to see us. They worked at the hotel and were eager to see the English band. We were equally eager to see them and made sure they all had our undivided attention! Even though Rick had his two girls lined up for the night, he just couldn't help himself taking one of them to one side and giving her the chat. Tony was too tired for small talk so he went back to his room. Me and Steve were now chatting up two lovely-looking girls; they spoke better English than us. They came from somewhere in Spain. We arranged to see them after the show, during which they were looking after the airlines guests. My girl's name was Calida, which means ardently loving, which I hoped she'd live up to. The only thing that put me off was the moustache under her nose, but other than that, she looked a fair sort. Steve's girl was Buena, 'the good one', which sounded promising for him.

We went back to our rooms, where I had my first experience of a proper shower, absolute heaven, better than a tin bath in front of a coal fire. I put on a white robe, courtesy of the hotel, and just relaxed with a Woodbine. The room was well tasty, and looking out at the Aegean Sea from my balcony I was living the dream. I ordered some sandwiches which came with some type of green grapes. Later I found out they were olives, and they gave me the trots. With a couple of nice cold Greek beers, I sat on the balcony enjoying every minute. We got down about half an hour before we started playing. We had another quick soundcheck and were ready to party. We'd bought some Farah hipster trousers, with white button-down shirts and slim knitted ties from Harry Fenton, and white winkle-pickers with zips up the side.

It was packed out in the club and it looked like the whole of the hotel had come to see us. We were going to start with 'Black is Black' by Los Bravos, then on to 'All or Nothing' by the Small Faces, and then 'I'm a Boy' by The Who. That feeling of waiting to play puts you on edge; we were up for it that night and couldn't wait – who wouldn't be, on the beautiful island of Rhodes, in a fantastic hotel, with an audience waiting for you to entertain them through the night? The first chord was struck and we were in, what a night. The sound system with its Marshall speakers was really good and the music we played was going down well. Everybody was dancing and having a great time. We finished the first set with 'Bus Stop' by the Hollies. When we came off we were sweating buckets and downed a few glasses of retsina. Lots of people came over and said they were enjoying our music, including Calida, who'd given the old moustache a bit of a trim. In fact, she looked a bit tasty and I was looking forward to having a drink with her later. We started the second set with our own material and got a good response. We had a whale of a time and got two encores, which is always nice. After the gig we had some of the local ouzo with Calida and Buena, and then walked along the beach with them. All we got was a snog, mind you. I'd this thing about her having a moustache, and I couldn't get my head around it. When I was snogging her, it felt a bit prickly above my lip, where she hadn't quite shaved it off properly.

I woke up next morning and the sun was already out in full force. I had breakfast with Tony and Steve; there was more fruit on the table than Spitalfields Market. Rick was having his bit of fruit in bed. This is where it's great being in a band, as everyone was coming up to us saying how much they'd enjoyed the show.

Before I came away, my old dad said,

'Make sure you're covered up when you go out into the sun. It's really strong and it'll burn you. Wear a hat and make sure you put plenty of suntan cream on.'

So I took this on board, as did Steve and Rick, but Tony decided he knew better. We had the whole day to ourselves. First off, we went out on a speedboat, driven by a local lad. Tony just had his trunks on and no protection. He was going home with a suntan and that was that. We had a great ride around the bay and were loving every minute of it. The other three asked the guy to stop the boat so they could have a swim in the sea. I'm a non-swimmer so I wasn't so keen. The three of them jumped in and were swimming like fish. If I can't touch the bottom then I don't go in, so I didn't. This guy fished out a kid's rubber ring from underneath his seat, which he gave me to put on. The other three were winding me up about not joining in. So like an idiot I put it on and jumped, well not so much as a jump, more like a gentle splash. So now I was giving it the big swim with my red rubber ring around me, when the guy took a couple of pictures of me with Tony's Kodak Brownie 127. They'd brought the kid's ring on board just to take the rise out of me. Rashly, I decided to take the ring off and show them I could swim without it – I couldn't. They pulled me out after I'd swallowed most of the Aegean Sea.

We had a great barbecue by the pool, which included fresh sardines. I'd only ever had cod, rock eel and nearly a pike before, so this was another first. We had a few beers and relaxed in paradise. Tony sat in a deckchair to top up his tan, while Steve sneaked off to see a girl he'd met from Canvey Island. It seemed a waste to come hundreds of miles to a foreign land and meet a bird who lives a few miles up the road to you. He came back an hour later looking very happy with himself, and plonked down on a deckchair for some sun.

I was just relaxing, having a beer and looking at the scantily dressed girls and taking it all in. I looked at Tony who was frying for England. Next thing Rick rushes up with a Spanish guitar borrowed from a member of the resident band.

'Quick,' he said, 'I've found a couple of French girls who I reckon are up for a serenade and a siesta in our rooms. Mine is Michelle and yours is Alice. They're real live wires. I'm going to sing 'Michelle' (the Number One hit with The Overlanders) to her, she'll like that. Do you know the chords to it?'

'I can get by,' I replied.

We shot off to see the two girls by the pool, well one of them was, her mate had gone for some fags. The one by the pool, Michelle, was ten out of ten. Rick was now giving it the big one, and started singing 'Michelle' to her. I got by with the chords and it sounded pretty groovy. Then her mate turned up, what a state! God hadn't been kind to her. She had this body that called out for help, and she was smoking those stinky Gitanes cigarettes. As soon as she saw me she latched onto me like a limpet. I know I sound horrible and I'm no Steve McQueen myself, but I'm sure she had webbed feet. Looking closer, she also had thick black hair underneath her armpits, but fortunately no moustache. I was lumbered, as Rick's Michelle wouldn't go anywhere without her mate, Alice. She certainly wasn't Alice in Wonderland, more like

Alice in No Man's Land. I had to tag along for Rick's sake and all I can say is that I did my duty!

The inevitable happened, Tony got sunstroke. The hotel had seen it all before and sorted him out before our final spot that night. He was as red as a beetroot and glowing. He downed pints of water and went and had a kip.

Steve reminded me that we'd a date with Calida and Buena after the gig and they were taking us to a local bar. I wasn't bothered about Calida, but Steve was smitten with Buena. They were like the bailiffs; they'd only come in twos, so I was lumbered. The night was a rave which included two fun songs, 'The Jolly Green Giant' by The Kingsmen and 'Mrs Brown, You've Got a Lovely Daughter' by Herman's Hermits. The best one of the night, which really went down well with the crowd, was 'It's Good News Week' by Hedgehoppers Anonymous, who were a group of RAF servicemen. It had been a great evening. The bonus was we weren't flying out until the next evening, so we had nearly a whole day on this terrific Greek island. We met up with the two girls and they took us to a local bar, which was a bit of a dump. One of the blokes there was drinking with his mates, and had previously been out with Buena, but we didn't know about this till later. He still fancied her, so when Steve tried to get his tongue down her throat, he didn't go a lot on that. It soon kicked off, as him and his cronies stood up and eyeballed me and Steve. They made a move towards us and it was time to leave. I grabbed Steve and he didn't need telling twice; we shot out of there like a couple of Roger Bannisters. When we got back to the hotel Steve went and did his own thing and I had a drink with some of the airline people.

The next day we had breakfast together on Rick's balcony. The girls from the airline got Rick a suite; mind you he had to keep them both sweet in another way. Tony had the look of a cooked lobster from his day in the sun. I was just scoffing my fourth croissant when Steve said,

'I had this foreign bird last night after I left you, she was rampant and couldn't get enough of me; the only thing that put me off, was the thick black matted hair underneath her arm pits.'

Well, the croissant got stuck down my throat and Rick choked on his fresh orange in a fit of giggles.

'What are you two laughing about? I didn't think it was that funny,' Steve said.

'Did she have funny feet?' I said.

'Well, yeah, it looked like she had webbed feet.'

Rick and me had to get out of the room, we couldn't stand it anymore; we were creasing up. Steve and Tony just looked at each other and put it down to too much retsina.

We were catching the plane back in the evening, so we enjoyed the last day. We played football with some other English blokes, and in the afternoon played against the waiters from the hotel on the sands. It did get a bit serious and there was nearly a punch-up over a penalty decision that went against them, given by one of their own. Anyway, I must add we won 3-1, a first on two accounts – we had played football and music in a foreign country.

We left the beautiful sunshine of Greece and flew into a storm when we got back to the UK.

♫ **21** ♫

Down and Nearly Out on All Fronts

Within a couple of weeks we had major issues. We continued with gigs all over the country, including Wolverhampton, Coventry, Bedford, Swindon, Cheltenham, Swansea and Cardiff. Then the wheels started to come off. As I said, we'd recorded a few numbers in a studio session that Pete had set up. The 45 rpm vinyl record with an extra couple of copies came back with only 'Suburban Mod' on it; Pete felt the other numbers we recorded were only average and not worth putting on. I must admit, seeing the label on the record with the name of your song on was a bit special. We thought Pete was going to do the business for us and try to place us with a recording company – this didn't happen. Then, disaster. Pete was offered a job in America with a similar music magazine offering him mega bucks; of course he took it. He'd left straight away and hadn't had time to contact any of the record companies. So we'd just lost the main man who could've got us in front of them. We were well annoyed and felt let down.

On top of it all my brother Arthur only got his girlfriend up the duff. My poor old mum was beside herself. In 1966 it was still a no-no to have a baby out of wedlock.

'It'll bring shame on our family's name,' my mum said. 'What will the neighbours think? I won't be able to face them in the street.'

'Didn't Sid offer you his weekend specials?' I asked Arthur. Do you know what he said, and he was well serious?

'They were too small when I tried to put them on.'

There wasn't much more to say after that. The baby thing went over my dad's head. He was more concerned about the local council knocking down his social club for a block of flats. So babies weren't a priority. His pint of beer and crib with his mates was number one on the agenda. The council weren't knocking his club down, that was for sure, he said.

'We've got to have a wedding straight away,' mum said.

'A feckin' wedding?' he replied. It was the first time I'd heard my dad swear at my mother. 'How can I think about weddings when all my army mates and me are going to lose our club? Get real, will you, Doris?'

'Don't you swear at me, Ron. You think more of your mates and that club than you do of your own family.'

Poor old mum, she was well upset and I had to have a word with my dad about his outburst. He said he was out of order and he'd make it up to her later. He then put on his bike clips and flat cap, and was off to his club. That night after his normal session with his mates, he said sorry to my mum and brought her in a bottle of Jubilee milk stout as a peace offering.

I was still seeing Anita, but not so often because of all the travelling with the band. When I got home one Sunday morning after travelling back through the night from a gig in Newcastle, the phone went – it was her. I knew by the tone of her voice this was a Dear John phone call. She'd met somebody else who she liked and it was unfair to him to have me in the background. So we were now just friends and that was all. I was well choked off and slammed the phone down like an idiot. I was tired after the long journey and couldn't think straight. What did I really expect? I was seeing other girls and I wanted to have it both ways. To be fair, we'd both said that we weren't joined at the hip and we could see other people if we wanted, although I did get the impression that she wasn't too keen on that idea.

'Suppose it makes sense,' she said.

Being me, I was playing the pop star card. I wasn't a pop star, that was for sure. I was one of many people in bands up and down the country looking for the big hit in the charts and stardom. We were a journeyman band just about keeping our heads above water. Sooner or later I'd have to get real. I'd just lost a girl who was 18 carat; there weren't many of them about, and it was all down to me.

When you get jilted you turn to your best mate. So after a kip I met up with Steve for a few beers. I told him about Anita and his reply was, 'More fish in the sea.' No sympathy from him, which, to be fair, I didn't deserve. At times like this you look for alternatives and after a quick pint, Steve's black book came out. There were a couple of old favourites who lived up the road. We'd agreed that if they or us hadn't pulled, we'd get in touch with each other. So it was a quick ring to Mandy to see if she and her mate, Viv, were at a loose end. As luck would have it, Viv was around Mandy's house and they were bored out of their brains. So we met up with them and went to see The Beatles' *A Hard Day's Night* at the Rex Picture Palace. It was an old pre-war building, and home to a family of bats, who kept flying around inside. They liked a good time, these girls, and we hoped we were going to have a good time with them later, if you know what I mean. So to impress, we supplied the du Maurier cigarettes, and two choc ices, which was really pushing the boat out. We had shown them a good time and hopefully they were going to show us their appreciation later. There's a saying that not all eggs hatch and that was so true in this case, as they both had the decorators in and that was the end of our anticipated night of lustful passion.

Later that week we went to the cemetery and visited the graves of Rod, Carol and Jimmy to pay our respects, and to remember what lovely people they were. It was a sad occasion and it gave me time to reflect on your own mortality, and how lucky you are that you can still breathe fresh air, while three of your close friends lay buried in front of you. Afterwards, we went back to the La Nero coffee bar where nearly all our long-term friendships had started. Everybody was there, including Steve, Tony and the lovely Diane, who now didn't have a boyfriend. Wendy and Roger were getting married next year, and they asked if we'd play at their wedding. I took the mick out of Roger and asked him where his briar pipe was.

'Don't talk to me about that, I'm still getting hallucinations even now.'

Alec had now joined his dad training greyhounds. The parties were still off at his place; the memory of the fire brigade had made sure his mum and dad had put an end to that. Ronnie turned up, he was now working for a farmer; I hope he had no pigs. Anne had really blossomed and was looking a bit of all right and she was free. I went to get the refills for everybody and thought, right, I'm in here. By the time I'd got back, my so-called best mate, Steve, had already got in there and asked her out, plus I still had to pay for all the espressos.

Not to be put off, I asked Diane out for a drink and she said yes. I was well chuffed and we both wondered why we'd never got together sooner. Unfortunately, she was off to America soon to see her brother Pete for a few weeks, so the relationship went on hold until she came back.

What followed next was going to tax the band's friend-ships and much more. Normally, Tony and Steve would come around to my house and we'd go in my car to Rick's, where the van and all the equipment were stored. Rick's dad had the transport yard with all his lorries next to his house, so we kept everything there for security reasons. We were playing in Canterbury in Kent that night, so we went over there about one o'clock in the afternoon to pick up Rick and the van. On our way we were overtaken by quite a few police cars that were on a shout. It's funny, but for whatever reason, police cars nearby always make you nervous. With this in mind Tony handed out the Craven 'A' fags. As we approached Rick's house it was like a scene from *Z Cars*. There were police everywhere and they were busy crawling all over Mr. B's lorries. We were stopped by a burly police sergeant from entering the yard, so we parked the car outside in the road and got out. He asked us why we were there. We explained why, but he didn't seem too impressed. We then saw Mr. B being taken away in handcuffs in a police car. Rick, looking visibly upset, came over to us and explained what had happened.

'They've taken dad down to the local police station.'

'What for?' I asked.

'Something to do with fraud and stolen property. They're going through our place like a swarm of locusts. Thank goodness, my mum's away at her sister's for a few days, or she'd have gone bloody mad at the way the police are going through our house.'

Then Mr. Diplomat Tony said, 'Is your dad at it, then?'

Rick just blanks him and said, 'We've got a problem. They won't release the Transit and all of our equipment has been impounded. Nothing's going anywhere today so we'd better let the agent know we can't do Canterbury tonight. They won't even let me use the phone at the moment, so we'll have to go to a phone box.'

'I'll go,' said Tony, 'anybody got any money for the call?'

I gave him the fourpence and he went and made the call. We walked down to the local El Cubano coffee bar to plot our next move. Tony came back after speaking to the agent who wasn't happy. We'd let him down twice and there wouldn't be a third time he said. Rick had spoken to his dad's brother; he was coming down from Ilford to sort things out and was bringing a solicitor with him.

We had jobs to fulfil and we'd no van, no amps, speakers or drum set. We all agreed that somehow we had to sort this out that day, as we were playing in Wickford the following night. Rick, even with all his grief, agreed to sing and not let us down. Steve's dad, who worked as a court usher, was going to contact the local police to see whether we could get our gear back. He had daily contact with the police in his job. Tony's younger sister Penny had a drum kit, so we could borrow hers. We knew all the other bands in the area, and we'd often help each other out if we could. Tony got in touch with the bass guitarist, Robin, from Johnny Brewster's band, which was still going strong.

'No problem,' he said, 'I'll find you some amps and speakers.'

By ten o'clock the next morning Robin brought the amps and speakers around. He said he needed them back by Saturday morning as they had a gig in Billericay that night. The van was more of a problem. I asked the secondhand car dealers I knew and one of Eddie's former mates said he had a runner, we could hire it for two quid a day. Me and Steve went to pick it up. It was an old Bedford Dormobile which had seen better days but it would do. So Tuesday night we somehow did the gig in Wickford. It wasn't one of our best performances, but we got by. We then did Ashford on the Wednesday, Maidstone Thursday and Ilford on the Friday.

Steve's dad came up trumps and managed to contact the officer in charge of Mr. B's case. By Friday night we had the van and all our gear back. Rick's dad was released on bail and we had a chat with him. In the nicest possible way he said he wouldn't be able to fund us any more or give us much help until the problem with the police was resolved. Also our roadie, Gordon, wouldn't be with us either as he had to unload some of his staff to cut costs until, hopefully, he was back in business. He wouldn't go into details and we didn't ask and really that was that. So we had no manager again. Pete had gone across the pond to the USA, and that virtually sealed our fate with the record companies.

What you have to appreciate is that bands were ten-a-penny, all trying to get a record deal and without a door opening you had no chance. So here we were, a jobbing band, travelling up and down the country, trying to make a living without any back-up. Tony once again took on the finances of the group; I worked closely with the agent to get the bookings. The agent, whose name was Art, had an office in Soho. He'd been fair to us, and we did feel a bit guilty in letting him down on those three gigs, but there was nothing we could do about it now. I did ask him if he could make the jobs more local to save on costs. He wasn't enamoured with that suggestion.

'You lot can't cherry pick what you want', he said. 'You either accept what I give you or not at all. There's plenty of other bands out there who want the work, so you should be grateful for whatever I give you.'

He was right, of course, and I'm sure all of us were wondering whether we should pack up.

So we were back on the road travelling all over the country. The money after expenses was virtually nil, you could earn more doing a paper round. I could just about afford a set of strings and a couple of plectrums for my guitar.

Steve kept going on about wanting to sing, he was moaning all the time about it. Reluctantly, we agreed he could do one number and only one. Steve's singing reminded me of Rick's former girlfriend, Andrea, at the posh party where we met. We had to pick the right gig. What better than a football club dance? We had one coming up in Islington in North London. He not only wanted to sing, but also play lead guitar on his own. Why we agreed to his request I don't know, we must have had a brain storm.

ಶಿ ಶಿ ಶಿ

We turn up and Steve is up for this booking. He's going to rock them in the aisles. Steve is a beer drinker like the rest of us, but tonight he's on the shorts. He's seen this gin advert with all these dolly birds dancing around, so he thinks it's cool and he's going to have some, and he did. We let him start the second set on his own. He won't tell us what he's going to sing, he says it'll be a surprise and it is. He's in a happy mood because his football team has had a right result today. He borrows my guitar and starts trying to re-tune it, which gives me the hump. The gin is giving him a glow now and he's full of himself. He goes up to the mic and gives it the big one. He looks back at us with a grin on his face, as we all sit down to listen to Elvis 'Steve' Presley. He starts singing, me and the other band members can't believe what he's doing. It's gone from a great evening to a Titanic disaster. The crowd are now hostile and looking to tear us apart. Steve is only singing 'I'm Forever Blowing Bubbles' to a crowd of Arsenal supporters. Anybody who knows about football knows that this is West

Ham's club anthem. We're playing in North London, which is Arsenal territory. West Ham is in East London and, of course, Steve is a Hammers fan. Somehow we are forgiven, after we tell them that Steve was once on the books of Arsenal as a schoolboy and he's only singing it as a wind-up. Fortunately, they believe us – being pissed out of their brains helped.

Steve didn't go near the gin again or the mic.

∂♥ ∂♥ ∂♥

We were rolling on with all the gigs, and it was taking its toll on everybody. We were all tired, and potless. We did try one or two record companies with our demo record, but couldn't even get through the door. We trawled a copy of the demo around with us, in case a record company came to one of our gigs, which they didn't, and we started to wonder where we were going and what we were achieving.

There was one funny night. We played a gig at a holiday camp at Seawick Sands, near Clacton. The town's a bit of a dive and some clown had altered the signpost to the Costa Del Seawick. We decided we were going to stay overnight here, as there were lots of holidaymakers, which meant girls, and they'd also got a great bar. So Rick brought this massive tent for us to sleep in under the stars. He'd got the tent off his sister, who was in the girl guides. You knew that, as it had 'Bentfield Girl Guides' stamped all over the tent. Before we started the gig we attempted to put the tent up at the holiday camp – that was a joke. In the end a couple of young lads put it up for us for a quid. The gig went well and we all got drunk afterwards and made our way back to the tent. It made a change not to have any girls with us; Newcastle Brown ales and Manikin cigars were our friends that night. We'd just got to kip when we heard noises and giggling. There were some blokes outside shouting,

'Come on, girls, let us in, we've got some drink for you and something else.'

Then more giggles and again some bloke said,

'Hope you've got your uniforms on, girls.'

That was too much for us and we flew out of the tent. Five blokes about our age were outside; they couldn't believe it when we appeared.

One said, 'You're blokes, we thought you were girl guides.'

We looked at each other in shock for a minute, and then looked at the tent with 'Girl Guides' stamped all over it. We all burst out laughing, and ended up having a beer with them.

Various things happened over the following two weeks. First, I got a mysterious phone call asking me to go to Chigwell in Essex to meet a manager of a band, but he wouldn't tell me the name of it. I was inquisitive, so I went with Steve. He went for a coffee while I visited this posh house, very near the great Bobby Moore's home. In his driveway was a top of the range Rolls Royce. He was a bloke in his thirties and was well switched on, you knew he wasn't a time-waster. We sat down over a coffee and he came straight out with it. The band he represented was quite high profile and played similar music to us but it was all their own material. They were in the papers a few weeks ago when one of the band members had died of a drugs overdose. He came straight to the point.

'Subject to meeting the other members of the band, I want you to join them as their lead guitarist. They've heard you play at a couple of gigs you did in East London and they liked what they heard.'

I was being offered a job in a Top 40 chart band; in fact they'd got to No.18 in the charts with their last number. The money was out of this world and they needed me straight away, as they were touring Scandinavia in six weeks' time and I'd have to learn all their numbers by then. I was well taken aback, especially with all the fringe benefits. I just sat there with my mouth wide open and couldn't think of anything to say. He wanted a decision within 24 hours and said,

'It's a no brainer, I'm offering you a massive opportunity to become a pop star with plenty of money, and playing venues you could only dream about.'

As I left him, I wondered why I hadn't taken his hand off there and then. On the way back home, I had a long chat with Steve who went very quiet as I told him.

After listening, he said, 'You've got to go for it, you'll be a mug if you don't. It's a once in a lifetime opportunity.'

When I got home, I had a chat with my dad who was listening to *Round the Horne* on the radio.

'As a career move it makes sense,' he said, 'with the opportunities it provides, and of course the money. On the other hand, you're in a band with your mates. They've the same goal as you, all trying to be successful. You either stick with them or leave and join a band that's nearly at the top of the tree already.'

It was a hard one to call. I asked Steve not to tell Tony and Rick, which he agreed to do. The only downside to the band, if the rumours were true, was that they had a drug culture, which wasn't for me. After a sleepless night I rang their manager to say, 'Thanks, but no thanks.' He thought I was mad, and I probably was. My thoughts were, I started with 'Modern Edge' and I wanted to be successful with them. Steve was well surprised I never took the job but was pleased I was still in the band. We never did tell Tony and Rick.

The following week another major problem reared its ugly head. Tony was rushed to hospital with appendicitis and had an operation straight away. At the time we were in between bookings, but had a few gigs coming up. We visited Tony in hospital and he'd got a ready-made replacement.

'My sister Penny,' he said. 'She practises with me all the time and knows most of the numbers we play. She's been playing drums longer than I have. Remember, my old man's played with the big bands as a drummer and still does a bit now. It's in our blood.'

'She's a girl,' said Steve. 'They can't play drums.'

'She can play alright, don't you worry about that,' replied Tony. 'Plus she left school a few weeks ago, and is waiting for a college place, so she's available.'

So that's what we did. We saw Tony's parents and they had no problem as long as we weren't staying away from home, which we weren't. Penny was up for it and over the next few days we practised with her. We needed some practice ourselves, so we didn't mind. She was a good little drummer and not a bad looking girl, which makes no difference at all, it's just a bloke thing. Tony would be off for about four weeks, so Penny was now very important to us. She was spot on with her drumming.

'Christ, she's better than Tony,' Steve said. 'I take it all back about girl drummers.'

The first gig with Penny was at a college with about 250 people there. As Penny was setting up her drum kit on stage, the students were taking the piss because she was a girl and playing drums. One of them said,

'What's your name – Honey?' (Ann 'Honey' Lantree was the drummer with the well-known group, The Honeycombs, who had a big hit with, 'Have I the Right'.)

I must admit there was an edge to this booking with Penny playing the drums. She was great, and one of her drum solos had everybody shouting out for more. Penny was a winner and it gave us a bit of an extra bounce; she played at all the venues until Tony came back. However, me and Steve were really pleased to have Tony back, as Rick was taking an unhealthy interest in Penny. We caught Rick looking at her when she bent over to fix her bass drum and you could see what he was thinking.

'Penny for your thoughts, Rick,' I said.

'She's got a lovely arse, hasn't she?'

'She's Tony's sister.'

'I know, but wouldn't it be nice.'

On Sunday nights we used to go to the Ilford Palais dance hall, where the Phil Tate and Nat Allen bands used to play. In the middle they had a big silver ball rotating from the ceiling. We had a spare Sunday, so me and Steve went up to the Palais for a laugh. We thought we looked the dog's bollocks with our new look, collarless granddad shirts, chisel-toed shoes and bell-bottom trousers. Sunday nights at the Palais were called 'grab a granny night'. For whatever reason, some of the girls were older than on other nights. The format was that the lights would go down really low where you could hardly see. The girls would be on the dance floor waiting for us blokes to ask them to dance. When the band started to play the blokes were on them, like rampant dogs, that's why it was called grab a granny. As it was dark, you didn't know who you were grabbing. They did this about three times a night; it was like pass the parcel but in reverse, if you know what I mean. First time around when the music started, me and Steve were on the dance floor in seconds. The first girl I pulled had a great body and was well tasty. When the lights came back on I asked her for the next dance and she refused.

'Why,' I said, 'what's wrong with me?'

She replied, 'I just don't fancy you, you look a bit shifty, sound common and you're not very good looking.'

Deflated, I had to go and sit down, light up a Woodbine, and have a couple of light ales in the bar on the strength of that. In fact I nearly went home.

Second time around, same format, lights out and the music started. I was in there, she had a flip hairstyle down to her shoulders, not a bad bum, but something didn't smell nice. Bleedin' hell, it was Old Spice – it was a bloke. He didn't seem to notice, as he was spaced out on drugs. Steve had pulled this little blonde who looked a bit special. As soon as Steve saw me with this bloke, he kept calling me Nicola. I wasn't happy. He'd pulled, and I was on my Jack Jones. There was only one more grab a granny turn that night, so I had to make it count. The music started, lights low and I'm in. One guy pushed me out of the way and grabbed this bird, leaving her mate on her own. I just saw the back of her, so I took a gamble and grabbed hold of her. It was a slow number so I held her a bit tight. The smell coming from her was heaven. She had Evening in Paris perfume on, which you could only get from Woolworth's (I'd bought Anita some.) We never said anything; we just smooched to the music and it felt nice. As soon as the music stopped she was on her way out. She gave me a peck on the cheek.

'It was nice dancing with you,' she said and she turned to leave.

'Can I give you a lift home?' I said.

'No, my dad's picking me up, so I've got to go now.'

'What's your name and telephone number?'

'It's Kathy, and unfortunately I'm not on the phone.'

'How can I get in touch with you?'

'I work at Leonard's in Romford. Ring me there,' and she was gone.

So I'm on my own, on my night off, but Steve has Jackie and he wants to take her home. She went to the toilet and Steve collared me.

'That Jackie is a bit of all right, do you fancy getting a ...'

'Stop there,' I said, 'I ain't getting a bus home, so forget it.'

'Oh, I said to her that I would take her home to Dagenham. Would you drive my motor then, Nick, so I can get in the back with her?'

'What am I, a poxy taxi driver?'

'Go on, mate,' he said. 'I'd do it for you, wouldn't I?'

So muggins has to drive his Ford Zodiac. Now to be fair it was a nice motor, but it did like a bit of petrol. You could only get about 17 miles to the gallon and we were always running out of petrol. So there I am driving, while Steve is trying to get his end away with Jackie. The noise coming from the back of the motor was like a zoo at feeding time. All that noise and effort, and all he got was a wet snog. We dropped her home in Dagenham and Steve made arrangements to see her again.

I heard a funny story about the Ilford Palais from one of my friends John. One of his mates lived a fair distance from the Palais. The bus service wasn't good, so he decided to take his Raleigh 3-speed bicycle with red frame, white mudguards and chain guard to Ilford. He met this girl who he really fancied and she invited him back home for coffee. Of course he'd got no car, and she was going home by bus. So it was agreed he'd follow the bus on his bike. Unbeknown to him, she lived seven miles away. It was a hot sultry evening, and he'd had to cycle his bollocks off on this Raleigh to keep up with the bus. You can imagine it, can't you? The bus stopped and the girl got off. In the distance she saw him on his bike peddling like Reg Harris towards her. He arrived totally knackered; his bri-nylon shirt was sticking to him with sweat after his seven mile bike ride.

She went up to him, sniffed and said,

'You stink like a polecat. I couldn't fancy you now, you'd better get back on your bike and ride home.'

Talking about Ford Zodiacs, there was a mate of ours called Des, who lived down the same street as us. He'd just passed his driving test and had bought this Zodiac. The bodywork was good, and it looked a fair motor, until he took me and Steve out for a ride in it. We went down to Ramsgate on a nice sunny day. Halfway down to the coast it started to rain; well, we thought it was rain. As Steve pointed out to Des,

'It's only raining on the front windscreen, nowhere else.'

We stopped the motor. There was a great big hole in the radiator and the water was cascading all over the windscreen. We stuck some bubblegum over the hole. About every ten minutes we had to fill it up with water as it was still leaking. We pulled into a garage to get some petrol, but Des's door wouldn't open, so he jumped over me to get out of my side. In doing so, the door on my side came away. It was a nightmare and we were glad to get home. Next day Des was giving this motor a right good shine and I was having a chat with him.

'Why shine it up before you take it down the scrappy?'

'Bollocks,' he replied, 'It's a nice motor, I'm giving it a right good shine because I'm taking my new tart out in it this afternoon.'

Next day I saw Des; he'd got a broken arm, cuts and bruises, was walking with a limp, and there was no Zodiac outside his house.

'What's happened, my son?' I said.

'What's happened? I'll tell you what's happened. I've got my bird in the motor and we're driving down the High Road in Manor Park, when this Morris Minor pulls out in front of me. I swerved and hit a Ford Anglia. It was unreal after that.

After I made contact with the Anglia, the motor split in half. I see my feckin' bird in one half of the motor, she's sails past me and hits a Mini. My half of the motor sails along for another few yards with me in it, and hits a lamp post.'

I'm absolutely creased up with laughter by now.

'I'm sorry, Des, but it is funny.'

'Feckin' funny,' he said. 'My bird's in traction in hospital, the motor's a write off, and so are the Mini and the Anglia. The lamp post's bent across the road, bloody chaos I'm telling yer. The Old Bill said my motor was a cut and shut, and that's why it split in two. Oh, yeah, and I wasn't taxed or insured.'

We weren't getting many bookings from our agent, so we were trying to get some ourselves. Rick's dad still had major issues with the police so he couldn't help much. We were getting tired, and a bit fed up travelling all over the country, earning washers and sleeping in the van overnight. We tried to get a manager to take us forward, but there were more sharks out there than the government.

There was one funny gig in London, we did a trade union dance, held in their own building; they'd converted the canteen to a dance hall for that one night only. As we were setting up, Tony had run a cable from a socket to one of our amps when this bloke came up to him.

'You can't do that here, mate. That has to be done by one of our own trade union electricians in this building.'

'You're having a laugh, ain't yer?' said Tony.

'No, they have to do it. We've got rules about things like this and we stick to them.'

'Fine, let him come and do it,' said Tony as he downed tools.

We had to wait while one of their brothers did the switch. We were late starting because of it, so we charged them another ten quid on top of our fee, as we were working an extra hour.

Unfortunately, things were going downhill, we just didn't have that edge anymore. We did a gig in Wisbech, said to be the capital of the English Fens, but it's still in the middle of nowhere! It was a Thursday night and raining cats and dogs. We put the radio on and listened to 'Last Train To Clarksville' by The Monkees. We felt this journey was the last train to nowhere. Have you ever been across the Fens when it's raining, cloudy, cold and misty? It feels like the end of the world. The van's heating was playing up and we were freezing our nuts off, plus we'd run out of fags. We got lost and asked this Farmer Giles character, who looked pie-eyed, where Wisbech was.

'Right,' he said, 'you go across this field, over the next meadow, turn left by Morris Farm.'

Before he could finish, Tony's lost it; he was sitting in the back with a raging toothache, and shouted out,

'Tell that feckin' twat does this look like a bleedin' tractor?'

We eventually found the dive we were playing at. It must have been the worst place we'd ever played. Only about 20 people turned up; because of the weather, we were told. There were more bum notes played that night than in all the years we'd been together. We got home about three in the morning. I'd never seen us all so down and depressed. The group was now disintegrating and we could see it was coming to an end. We'd tried to make it, but it wasn't going to happen, so maybe it was about time we called it a day.

The next night's gig, on the Friday, also involved water. We were playing on West Mersea Island, near Colchester. The gig was going well until a bad storm hit the island and everybody went home; we thought it was because of the storm, but no, coming into Mersea you have to go over a tidal causeway. As we made our way out of Mersea the tide was in, which made the causeway impassable for about an hour. That's why everybody went home early to miss it, except for us four dickheads. Saturday, we didn't have a booking, which was unusual, but we had one on the Sunday night in Norwich, which was a bit of a trot.

On the Saturday morning my mum brought me up a nice cup of Lyons tea, two slices of Marmite toast and my musical paper. She was much happier now, it had been a false alarm about Arthur's girlfriend being up the spout. I open up the newspaper and there's a picture of the band I'd turned down. Their new release was rising fast in the charts and they were taking the pop world by storm. I was well choked off but it was my own fault. I had the opportunity but decided to stay with my mates. Later that day Steve phoned to say he was seeing Jackie, the girl he met at the Ilford Palais a couple of weeks ago, so he wouldn't be seeing me tonight. I was thinking to myself it can't get any worse, I've lost the opportunity to be in a chart band, my best mate has lined himself up, and Diane is still in America.

I hadn't made contact with Kathy, who I'd met at the Ilford Palais, as I'd been playing with the band every night. So I decided to give her a bell at Leonard's, which was a large department store. When I got through I asked for Kathy. The girl just laughed,

'We've got six Kathys here. What's her surname?'

I didn't know so I thought I'd shoot up to Leonard's and find her. I had no petrol in the motor, so I jumped on the 247A bus and went to Romford. It was a big store and I trawled around the different departments looking for her. I'd done them all, except for the lingerie department. Blokes ain't very brave about girls' underwear. We love the suspenders, stockings, colourful bras and knickers. But most blokes will just bung their girlfriend a few quid to buy them, hinting at the ones they like, which are usually the most uncomfortable to wear. They haven't got the bottle to go in and select them, especially when the sales lady asks what size they want. I crept into the lingerie department trying to find Kathy. She was behind the counter serving a customer, so I hung about like a bad smell, hiding behind a row of 38B cups until she had finished serving. Then a lady assistant tiptoed up on me and frightened me to bleedin' death.

'Can I help you, sir?'

I went red and started waffling to her. Finally I got it out about Kathy.

'She's a bit busy at the moment. Come back in about half an hour when she goes for her lunch.'

I came back as she was leaving to go to the staffroom for her break. She was well surprised to see me. She looked a bit of all right and had a sense of humour, especially when she thought the 38B was a bit too big for me. I loved her geometric hairstyle, modelled on the Vidal Sassoon look. She had an hour for lunch, so we went to the nearby Mocamba coffee bar, and had a couple of milk shakes and a sandwich. The Seeburg jukebox was playing 'Sha La La La Lee' by the Small Faces. She was really friendly and we got on well. Kathy was 20 and lived locally with her parents. She didn't have a boyfriend at the moment because the last one and the others before were only interested in one thing, and not her as a person. Hearing that, I nearly walked the walk, but she did seem to have a nice personality and a sympathetic ear, which I was sorely in need of.

'Would you like to come out tonight?' I said.

'I would have loved to but I've got to go to a family gathering, it's for my grandad's 80th birthday. What about next Saturday? There's supposed to be a great band playing at the Dagenham Assembly Rooms,' she said.

'I've heard about them. How about I meet you outside there about 6.30, then?'

'I'll look forward to that,' she said.

I should've heard of them – it was us who were playing there. So I had a night in, watching Patrick Macnee and Honor Blackman in *The Avengers*.

As I said we were playing at Norwich the following day, then Ely, Ipswich, Sudbury and Clacton which took us through to Friday, and then the gig at Dagenham on the Saturday.

We were still sleeping in the van while we were away, we just couldn't afford the lodgings, and in fact we nearly didn't have a van at Ipswich. We'd unloaded the gear into the dance hall. We only had about two bob between us so we bought some sausages, and because it was raining outside we cooked them on a little camping stove in the van. While they were cooking, a couple of girls came over to us for a chat, and we joined them in the doorway of the dance hall. We were so engrossed in chatting them up and scrounging fags that we forgot all about the sausages. One of the girls said,

'Is there meant to be smoke coming out of the back of your van?'

It was too late, there was a bang and the back windows of the van shot out. The glass and the Walls pork sausages came out like rockets, and nearly took our bleedin' heads off. So, no more cooking in the van. We had to put an old curtain across the back where the windows were supposed to be to keep the draught out. We were thinking it couldn't get any worse, when the next day a brace of pheasants were on a suicide mission and hit the windscreen while we were driving. Fortunately, they only cracked it; mind you it was some crack as when it rained, water would pour through. The only bonus was that we sold the pheasants for a shilling each to a butcher in Sudbury. The van was falling to bits and when we played that night, a crowd of pikeys came over to us and took the right piss out of our beaten up old van. They walked around it and one of them said,

'Why don't you come and join us at our camp, you're one of us now.'

At the Clacton gig we arrived there in the early afternoon. As we had no money, and a couple of hours to spare, we managed to bunk into the local flea pit, as we used to do as kids. The film was *Alfie* with Michael Caine. After the film we all thought we were Alfie, but soon realised we weren't, as we couldn't pull a skin off a rice pudding that night. Well, Tony did, she was an oddball even for him. She had this black cape wrapped around her, a pair of old army boots, and a witch's hat; we thought it was Halloween. In the end he decided he was too tired to chase her around the camp fire and we all drove back down the A12 and home.

On the Friday we were playing at a wedding in Hackney, East London. You've heard of weddings from hell, well this was one of them. It was one of Tony's ex girlfriends, Rosie, who was getting married, not a good start. She still held a torch for him or more like something else. Where we were playing was a bit rough and you couldn't let the gear out of your sight for a minute. Rosy was a real East End girl and was tattooed up like a beauty, and every other word she said was an F.

'What made you go out with her,' I said to Tony, 'she looks like hard work.'

'Rosie has a heart of gold, really,' replied Tony,' but a mouth as big as the Blackwall Tunnel.'

'When you first met her, what was the attraction?'

'She was a good bunk up,' he said.

There was no answer to that. Rosie was marrying a bloke from Middlesbrough. She'd met him when she went to visit her previous boyfriend, also from East London, in Durham prison. He was serving three years for a robbery in Sunderland. After the visit she went into a local pub for a pint of Newcastle Brown, as you do, and met this bloke. A few months later she was expecting a sprog and was now marrying him. In the meantime her previous boyfriend came out of jail and was not happy with her marrying the bloke from up north, especially as she was now expecting his kid. You could see at some point it was all going to kick off. Tony was invited to the wedding, held in the local registry office, and had asked us to come for moral support, which we did as he was a mate. So we've Rosie who's well up the duff and her family from London on one side, and this bloke from Middlesbrough and his family on the other. Rosie's family were not happy with her marrying a bloke from up north, and you could feel the tension in the air. The bridegroom was nicknamed Mo. When the registrar was doing the ceremony bit, he said,

'Will you, Morris Cuthbert Louis Sedgwick take Rosemary Smith ... ?'

The laughter from Rosie's family at her future husband's name was wicked; his family were clearly not happy at having the piss taken out of their man.

Well it rapidly went downhill after that. We were playing at the reception when there was a bundle and a half. The fight started on three fronts. Rosie's former boyfriend turned up unannounced, with some of his mates. He looked like

Charles Atlas, so there was only ever going to be one winner. Mo's family and Rosie's family were having one almighty punch-up, when the police turned up; we threw our gear into the van and made haste. What a night! We didn't even get paid for it.

The week on our mini East Anglian tour was the tour that broke the camel's back for all sorts of reasons. We'd lived in and out of the van all week, as we'd done for the last few months. We'd all had enough after well over two and half years of playing full-time all over the country. After the next night's gig at Dagenham we'd agreed to have a final chat to discuss where we were going. We hadn't fallen out with each other and were still great mates, but the time had come to maybe move on to pastures new. So next week, decision time. Steve was taking Jackie to the Dagenham gig. We got there early and set up. We'd played there before and it was normally a good night. We decided to play mostly covers as sometimes it's best to play numbers that people can connect with and tonight was one of those nights. We did a soundcheck about six and were ready for 7.30 when the dance started. I was waiting for Kathy outside, as people were coming into the hall. At 6.30 sharp she was there and she'd made a real effort to look nice. She had these hot pants on with a tight top. I couldn't take my eyes off her outfit, and the body which it was hugging. She seemed well pleased to see me and she gave me the 3/6d entrance fee to get in. For a moment I nearly took it, I was that skint.

'No,' I said, 'We don't have to pay.'

We walked through, everybody acknowledging me as a band member.

'How come you're getting all this attention?' Kathy said.

'Well, meet the lead guitarist of tonight's band.'

'What, you're a member of Modern Edge? I don't believe it, why didn't you tell me?'

'I just thought I'd surprise you.'

'You've certainly done that.'

'Look, I can't be with you on the dance floor, but hopefully you'll still have a great time.'

Steve introduced his girl Jackie to Kathy and they hit it off straight away. When we started playing I looked down at the dance floor, and I could see Kathy and Jackie dancing together and waving to us; it looked like they were really enjoying the evening. We played a few new numbers including a really funny one called 'They're Coming to Take Me Away, Ha-Haaa!' by Napoleon XIV. It went down a real scream. We had a fab night and the crowd wouldn't let us get off the stage. After the gig I took Kathy home, and she invited me in for a coffee. This was a real bonus I wasn't expecting. We had to keep quiet as her parents were fast asleep upstairs. We gave the coffee a miss and got straight on the settee. Kathy was up for it and so was I, the trouble was that the old settee wasn't, it kept squeaking every time you moved on it. Then her dad bellowed out,

'Kathy, who've you got down there?'

Course, he had to come down and investigate. He took one look at me and that was enough. He looked a real brute; I got up quickly and left straight away.

Next day, we got a phone call from Mandy and Viv, who we'd taken to see *A Hard Day's Night*. They were fed up, and hadn't had any attention paid to them lately. Fortunately we weren't seeing Kathy and Jackie tonight. Viv's mum was a bit of a girl; she was over 40 with bleached blonde hair and wore miniskirts that barely covered her arse. She was separated from her third husband and played the field. One bloke she'd met had a heart attack on the job. When the ambulance men turned up, she said to one of them,

'I didn't know I was that good.'

Steve had an empty house so we were up for it. Mandy and Viv were now sporting ultra short hairdos modelled on the Twiggy look, which suited them both. They were also wearing these black Go-Go boots which were low heeled, and just above the ankle, and Baker Boy caps. With their short miniskirts and low tops, they looked really tasty. The four of us enjoyed a very rewarding and exhilarating couple of hours washed down with Watney's pale ales and Pink Lady champagne for the girls, complements of Steve's mum and dad's cocktail cabinet. Steve later got an enormous bollocking for nicking his mum's champagne.

The Dagenham gig, where we'd been given a great reception, rekindled the spirit in the band, and we were going to have one more try for the big time. We were hoping perhaps that Rick's dad would come good again. Unfortunately, this wasn't going to be the case, as he'd been charged with fraud and tax evasion. This had a really bad effect on Rick as he was close to his dad. Then out of the blue our agent Art phoned me up.

'I'm going bust and I'm letting you know before the shit hits the fan. I'll be making a comeback later, but under another name, so we'll keep in touch.'

Normally, when this happens they don't tell you and you can run for the money they owe you. The reason for this was that his wife was divorcing him and she was trying to screw him for every penny he had. I think he'd been doing his own screwing, as he seemed very close to one or two of the girl singers on his books. He was sending a cheque for the money he owed us, which wasn't a lot. He added that he was doing this as sooner or later we'd make it and he'd still like to be our agent when that happened. To be honest we weren't that close to him and he could've done a runner with our money, so we were grateful for that. He gave me a list of our outstanding gigs and contacts so we could go direct to them and collect the money ourselves. He said it hurt him to do this but his wife was checking on his every move and had hired a private detective. He had to be seen to go skint and then keep a low profile for the next few months. He wished us luck and said he'd be back in contact as soon as possible.

We met up at the La Nero coffee bar and just about had enough money for the coffees. Tony took charge and we looked at every avenue open to us. There were about ten more gigs to do and they were all quite local, which meant there was no sleeping in the van. All our dreams had started at the La Nero in 1964 and it now looked like this was where it was all going to finish at the end of 1966. Ted, who was still the guv'nor, could see we were down and brought us over some more coffees on the house, which we appreciated. After much debate we decided to finish the band full-time after the last gig, and have a final one, back at La Nero. We would have a rest and then maybe go part-time for local gigs, which meant finding full-time employment again. After the decision was made, we felt a bit of a relief but there was a tinge of sadness as we felt we'd failed as a band, but we'd given it our best shot. I was even more gutted when the band I turned down was on *Top of the Pops*, but that's life, and there's nothing you can do about it.

The outstanding gigs had to be played and we got back to enjoying them again as we knew we'd made the right decision, even though we were extremely disappointed in not achieving our goal. We organised the last gig at La Nero and invited everyone we knew.

♫ 22 ♫

The Last Gig

Our last gig as a professional paid band was at Harwich in north Essex, where the nearest major town is in Holland! The van was now on its last legs, and we were dumping it the next day – it was a death trap. The windscreen had finally fallen out the night before at a dance in Basildon, so we were glad it wasn't raining. We'd all found some form of employment. Tony was going to work at a new musical shop that had just opened in Romford; Rick was helping his dad, still facing legal action; Steve was back fitting tyres; and I got a job selling cars again.

We arrived at the gig and were greeted by the manager of the hall. Harwich didn't get too many bands, so there was a full house that night. We unloaded the gear, set up and did our usual soundcheck. All was in order so we went outside, lit up one of Rick's Strand cigarettes and watched all the crumpet coming in. There seemed to be three girls to every bloke and the miniskirts were getting shorter. There were some right darlings coming in and we all felt a good night was on the cards, but for me and Steve this was off limits. We'd both agreed that Jackie and Kathy were owed a bit of loyalty and other girls wouldn't be on the agenda. But we couldn't resist chatting to the birds flocking around us; some looked as if they hadn't seen a bloke in years, but sadly we were going to have to disappoint them. The other two were eyeing up who they fancied. They wanted to make sure that they'd pulled before we started playing, so they'd someone lined up after the gig. Rick straight away went for this dark-haired girl who looked well tasty. Tony was back on oddballs, and pulled a bird that looked like she needed a blood transfusion.

Tonight we'd decided we were going to play a lot of the numbers the band had written including 'Suburban Mod', the number that me and Steve had written. The place was packed to the rafters and we were ready to go. The first set was all covers, the second all our own material. We thought even if they didn't like them, we did, and it was our last gig. The first set included 'Please Please Me' by The Beatles; 'The Crying Game' by Dave Berry; 'Everything's Alright' by the Mojos; 'Juliet' by The Four Pennies; 'Baby Please Don't Go' by Them; and 'Wonderful Land' from The Shadows, which I really enjoyed playing. The first set was as good as it gets, we were on top form. During the break we asked ourselves why we were packing it in, but bills had to be paid and we just weren't earning the money. The second set was going to be a different matter; we could go down like a lead balloon, as the revellers wouldn't have heard any of the numbers before but what did it matter, they wouldn't be seeing us again. What happened next completely overwhelmed us. The reception for our own numbers was tremendous. They loved them and wanted more, and they got more, because we were having a great time and could've played all night. We were supposed to finish at 10.30 but with all the encores we didn't finish till 11.30. The manager of the dance hall said, 'I would've been lynched if I'd tried to stop it!' He said our band was one of the best he'd heard, and we were welcome to play there anytime.

As we were putting our gear into the van a bloke of about 30 with long ginger hair down to his shoulders and wearing National Health glasses came up to me,

'You certainly had them rocking tonight, have you any tapes of the band? I'll return them to you, of course.'

I was really tired and it was nice to get a thank-you, but all I wanted to do was to get home. We must have been exhausted as Tony and Rick didn't even bother to meet the two girls they'd pulled. We had a few copies of the vinyl somewhere; I scrambled about in the van and found one under one of the seats together with some copies of the *Beano* and *Dandy*, mouldy sandwiches, an old packet of Senior Service and an empty Pepsi Cola bottle. We always carried a vinyl with us in case there was any interest from record companies, which there hadn't been. I handed the bloke the vinyl and wrote my address down on the packet of Senior Service. I found a fag inside before I gave it to him, and lit it up. He promised he'd return the vinyl. I should've asked him who he was but at that moment I couldn't have cared a monkey's.

On the way home it poured down with rain, and with no windscreen we all got soaked through. What a way to finish your last professional gig. You could see all the boys thinking of what could've been. What we did have was a great bond between us, and we'd never let each other down. We'd got some great memories and we'd played all over the UK and Greece. The very last gig at La Nero's was in a week's time and we were starting our new jobs the following week.

A few days later, me, Steve, Jackie and Kathy went for a drive. Steve had borrowed his dad's Vauxhall Victor. His dad had fitted a brand new eight-track stereo cartridge player which was the good news, the bad news was he only had a Matt Monro cassette. It was a cold December day with a beautiful blue sky, and we decided to go to Walton-on-Naze, near Clacton. We liked going there because you could play football on the Naze, walk along the beach with your bird, lie down on the sands, tell her how much you loved her, and then if your luck was in maybe a bit more. I must admit I really liked Kathy, she was a fun girl. We arrived and had a bacon sarnie at the café on the Naze. We had our game of football, the last time we saw our brown leather ball – I gave it the big one and it landed in the sea, and was now making its way to Holland with the outgoing tide. It was too cold for a snog on the beach so we switched on the radio and found one of the pirate radio stations. It was playing 'Life's Too Good to Waste' by Tony Christie. We lit up one of Steve's Park Drive cigarettes and enjoyed the record. After the record finished the DJ said, 'Listen to this great new record, and after I've played it I want your help.' The record came on and after a few seconds, Steve said,

'Bleedin' hell, that's 'Suburban Mod'!'

We couldn't believe it. We were mesmerised listening to ourselves on the radio and the girls said, 'It sounds great'.

When it had finished the DJ said,

'What do you think? What a great record and it's only a demo disc. I saw this top new Mod band a few days ago at a gig in Harwich, they let me borrow the record, but I've lost their address, does anybody know where they live? They're called 'Modern Edge' and they're from Romford, and I believe they'll be the next big group on the pop scene. This number, 'Suburban Mod', is a classic and it's my record of the week, it will certainly be getting plenty of plays on this station. Believe it or not, they haven't got a record deal. Can you believe that? Remember the name 'Modern Edge', and you've heard it here first on the good ship Radio North Essex with John Boy Gibson.'

Me and Steve never said a word for a minute; we were totally gobsmacked and lost for words until Kathy said to me,

'Well, you won't want to know me, now.'

'That's right,' said Jackie, 'We'll be surplus to requirements.'

We hugged the girls, and ran around the motor jumping for joy like a couple of idiots. We'd dreamed of this day since we were kids. We'd travelled thousands of miles, and played hundreds of gigs all over the UK. It was great to get some form of recognition at last. This radio station had started the ball rolling and it was gathering speed by the hour, we didn't know how to handle it. The station was inundated with requests asking where they could buy the record from. The calls came from all parts of the UK and Northern Europe, anywhere that could tune into the station.

The next day various record companies tried to get in touch with us, they were even turning up at our doorstep asking us to sign with them. I rang Diane in America and told her what was happening. Within 48 hours she and Pete were back in the UK to help us. The band met up with Pete at my house. My mum still served Camp coffee; I didn't have the heart to tell her it was horrible and I wished she'd buy that modern Maxwell House stuff. Pete was now one of the top music journalists in America and knew everybody in the business. He was great to us, and spent a lot of time making sure we were represented by a reputable company, who hopefully would be able to clinch us the right record deal and take the band forward to success and stardom. The thought of riding high in the charts with 'Suburban Mod', with tours being planned for all over the UK, Europe and America, was our dream come true.

Rick's dad was found not guilty. Hopefully when we began to earn all this money, we'd pay him back all that we owed him, as well as our own parents of course. We hoped that if we made it we could use his company to transport our equipment around the globe. We also wanted to get Big Al back on board, as we were going to need a road manager and security; it would be great to have him back in the team.

I'll stop here; there are so many more stories to be told about our adventures with 'Modern Edge', so watch this space.